Snuggled

THE 'D' #5

CHARITY PARKERSON

PUNK & SISSY PUBLICATIONS

Copyright

The scanning, uploading, and distributing of this book via the internet or via any other means without the permission of the copyright owner is illegal and punishable by law. Criminal copyright infringement, including infringement without monetary gain, is investigated by the FBI and is punishable by up to 5 years in federal prison and a fine of $250,000. Please purchase only authorized electronic editions, and do not take part in or encourage

—Warning: This book is intended for readers over the age of 18. Some of my books contain allusions to past abuse and trauma. I try to never have anything triggering on page and treat every situation with care.

Editor: BZ Hercules & Consultants

Contents

Introduction

Finley isn't looking for a new Little. Grayson isn't giving him a choice.

A year ago, Finley lost the most precious thing to him: his Little. Since then, he's moved over a thousand miles away, set up a new practice, and is trying to start over. He had accepted his life would be quiet from now on. Then Silas stepped in and now Finley can't stop going to the lavish invite-only parties and staying all night. It has nothing to do with the flowing alcohol or blatant debauchery. He's there for one reason: Grayson.

Grayson has been going to Silas' parties for over a year. He likes the freedom of being himself in a crowd. Grayson doesn't have that luxury in other aspects of his life. Even though men attempt to catch his attention at the wild gatherings, Grayson hasn't been interested in anyone until now. Unfortunately, Finley doesn't feel the same.

Despite giving Grayson his constant attention, Finley has no intention of replacing the man he lost and vowed to love forever. But life doesn't care about his plans, and neither does Grayson.

Chapter One

At only three years old, Grayson had lost his parents. Not only had his adult brother been the only person left to take Grayson, but Jacob was also the person who Grayson's parents had named to be his godfather. Jacob, being a famous actor on a very popular sitcom being filmed in New Orleans, had reluctantly accepted his role. It had always been Jacob's position that as long as Grayson had a roof, clothing, and went to school, his responsibility was met. He had possessed an extreme get-him-to-eighteen mentality. To be fair, Jacob had only been nineteen when he found himself in charge of a three-year-old. But Jacob had continued living his life while Grayson had been horribly neglected. It wasn't something Grayson had realized at the time. He had thought everyone lived as he did: completely alone.

Grayson had been too young at the time to remember his parents for long, and no one had been around to discourage him from an attachment to his favorite blanket that had quickly lost his mother's scent. When he started school, he was never bullied—since Jacob ensured Grayson had the best of all material things—but he didn't have friends either. The cycle of neglect and deep loneliness continued.

Grayson had been lost to the background.

At twelve, Grayson had stuffed his blankie in his backpack and taken a streetcar to the mall to pick out his Halloween costume alone, as he did every year. While inspecting all the popular themes for the year, Grayson kept returning to two: a plush dinosaur costume and a giant baby. Both costumes seemed way out of his age, but they came in his size. Grayson had bought both.

When Halloween rolled around, Grayson had nervously donned the dinosaur costume and slipped from the house. He prayed every step he wouldn't see anyone he knew. The first doorbell he rang, Grayson wondered if he would puke. He felt like a baby in an outfit most kids his age would die before they wore. Then the door had opened and a woman—who Grayson imagined would be his mother's age— looked at him. A bright smile lit her face. She squealed in delight. For fifteen minutes, she had gushed over Grayson's costume. Then, after learning Grayson was alone, she had left her husband to hand out candy while she accompanied Grayson from door to door. It was the first time in memory Grayson had anyone's attention. Now, at twenty, Grayson was who he was. That night had changed him, or perhaps it had simply shown him who he was. Either way, Grayson was here: Silas' party.

He had attended his first event over a year ago and hadn't stopped since. Silas D was a rich man who seemingly had nothing better to do than look out for people like Grayson. People with kinks. Even if Grayson had never really gotten to explore those kinks, he was well aware he was different. Three weeks ago, Grayson had gone from being a party guest to becoming a house guest when Silas' husband, Benji, took pity on Grayson and asked him to move in. Grayson was more grateful than he could articulate. Even though Grayson had received the remainder of his parents' estate at eighteen, Jacob had also practically marched Grayson from his home, his obligation completed. For the past two years, Grayson had struggled at being an adult. He wasn't poor. It wasn't as if Jacob had kicked him into homelessness. Grayson just wasn't very good at being an adult. The only time he felt like himself was at Silas' parties. Every other day, he wore a mask. Living with Silas meant freedom. He got to be himself every day, and no one batted an eye.

Still, Grayson was an anxiety-ridden mess from years of neglect. He watched Benji with Silas, and he wanted that for himself. His heart ached with a desperate need to be snuggled and kissed. To be more than accepted but to be loved as himself. Because of Benji and Silas, Grayson knew there were people out there who might want him as is. The problem was, there was only one person Grayson was interested in, and Grayson didn't think Finley wanted anything more than to be friends.

Finley had eighteen years on Grayson. Grayson didn't give a shit about any of that nonsense. Finley's dark red hair and light green eyes, combined with his sexy Scottish accent, always made

Grayson blush. To be fair, Grayson always blushed. Did he mention he was a mess? Finley also had this wide chest that looked perfect to sleep on and a cuddly-looking body. Jesus, he made Grayson dream. Nights like tonight, where they sat side by side, Finley's closeness made Grayson burn.

Finley had shown up for a few minutes over a month ago for one of Silas' parties. For the two parties since, Finley had stayed the whole night in the play area with Grayson. They colored together and talked some. Never about anything important, but it was nice. Finley smelled like expensive cologne. His scent always beckoned Grayson closer. Still, Grayson hadn't gotten the nerve to start a conversation. He always responded to Finley's questions and listened while Finley spoke, but

Grayson didn't know what to say to someone like Finley. He was a neurologist and super smart. Grayson was just Grayson. He had never been special.

"I've been wanting to ask you something."

At Finley's admission, Grayson scooted closer, even though he couldn't seem to meet Finley's stare tonight. He kept coloring in his coloring book, hoping his move gave Finley the hint he was listening. Grayson was always listening. He just didn't have much to say.

Thankfully, Finley took the nudge. "I was wondering if you'd possibly want to do something with me outside these parties... like go to lunch?"

At the question, Grayson found the courage to meet Finley's stare. As always, when their eyes met, Grayson felt like a different person. It was a bit addictive. "Okay."

A sweet smile touched Finley's lips. "Good. I guess I should get your address or phone number so we can make plans."

"I live here."

Finley blinked. "You do?"

Grayson's nervousness returned at Finley's open surprise. He must look like such a loser compared to the men Finley interacted with daily. Grayson went back to coloring so the hood of his bunny pajamas would hide his face. He could feel his cheeks heating. Anxious tears pressed at the backs of his eyes. He hadn't liked anyone at all in a long time. Not like Finley. Grayson hadn't bothered with letting any crushes grow because he was different. He had to keep his secrets. Most people wouldn't accept him for himself.

"Well, I guess that makes you easy to find," Finley said, making it easier for Grayson to breathe. "Do you have a number?"

Grayson dragged his backpack closer and dug out his phone. Even though he sat there dressed as a Little, Grayson still felt a bit strange as he unlocked his phone and passed it Finley's way. The device had a protective cover that was bright pink with push-pop bubbles and cat ears. He usually took off the case before using it in public. In this instance,

Finley was acutely aware of Grayson's quirks. It seemed ridiculous for Grayson to hide them now.

Finley didn't as much as blink as he took the phone and clicked around. His phone buzzed and Finley typed in both devices, sending messages back and forth between them.

He passed Grayson's phone back. "There. Now we can talk anytime."

Grayson checked his messages. Finley had added himself as a contact. He read the messages Finley had sent between their phones.

Grayson: *This is Grayson's phone.*

Finley: *This is Finley's. Let's be friends.*

Grayson bit his lip, trying to squash a smile as he sent Finley a text of his own before putting the device back in his backpack.

Grayson: *I'd like that. Text me when you get home.*

When Finley's phone buzzed again, a deep chuckle rumbled from Finley's chest. Grayson fought a sigh. He just genuinely liked everything about Finley, but Grayson didn't understand why Finley spent time with him. There was nothing special about Grayson. He didn't think he was even particularly cute.

"Are you telling me to leave?"

Grayson's chin shot up at Finley's question. Their gazes met again. Finley was mesmerized by him every time. "No. I just meant I'm not ready to stop talking to you for the night."

"Have you started talking to me for the night? I hadn't noticed."

Grayson blushed. He knew he wasn't very good at this. "I'm sorry."

A line appeared between Finley's eyebrows. "Why are you apologizing?"

Grayson shrugged. "It's not that I don't want to talk to you. I don't know what to talk about. You're probably friends with a lot of smart people." Grayson couldn't believe he said that last part aloud.

Finley was back to blinking at him.

Grayson didn't know why he always had to be so dumb. "Sorry."

They stared at each other for a minute.

Fear washed over Grayson. He didn't want Finley to leave because he realized Grayson likely wasn't his type. Grayson held his crayons out to Finley. "Do you have a favorite color?"

A smile snapped to Finley's lips. "Green."

Grayson nodded and handed the green crayon to Finley. "You can color the grass. Mine is blue. I'll color the sky."

They bent over the coloring book. Their faces were so close, all Grayson had to do was turn his head and he could kiss Finley's cheek. Before he could stop himself, that was exactly what Grayson did.

Finley froze.

In his fear, Grayson dropped his voice to a whisper. "Thank you for being my friend." He went back to coloring while praying Finley didn't leave now. Life had been incredibly lonely. For the first time, he saw a slight glimmer of hope.

The grand parties Silas threw one or two times a month weren't really Finley's thing. He wasn't much of a drinker. There was no way in hell he would put a collar on some poor guy and force him to his knees. Until meeting Grayson, he hadn't thought Silas' parties had anything to offer him whatsoever. Now he couldn't stop showing up. When he wasn't there, all he did was think of Grayson. He needed answers. There had to be a reason for this fascination. Maybe he just needed to know why Grayson always apologized and rarely met his eye. His every action screamed he had suffered a lifetime of abuse. That didn't sit well with Finley. Finley couldn't leave the man alone.

Grayson was a tiny guy with soft-looking blond curls and sweet green eyes. He was the absolute picture of youth and innocence. Finley always wanted to tell him he had no business at Silas's, but Finley had no right to do so. So Finley came every time he was invited and spent the entire night at Grayson's side. If he couldn't make Grayson leave, he would keep him safe. Finley didn't think there was a soul there who would treat Grayson with the care he obviously needed.

Tonight, he had gotten Grayson's number and made a decision. He would take Grayson to do things outside the occasional party. He hoped if Grayson saw he could be accepted outside these lurid gatherings, then he would search for a better way to find comfort. Finley had a bad feeling in his gut about Grayson being left alone at those events. Grayson needed a friend. A protector. At least, that was what Finley told himself as he drove home. His feelings were completely innocent. They were no more than friends.

As Finley stripped away his tie and jacket, he fought against the images in his head. They poked holes in his claims of friendship. Grayson was a temptation Finley hadn't experienced in a long time. Not since Coby died. Just the thought of Coby killed every hint of desire. They had been together for eight years. Seven of those, they had been married. Finley had never been happier in his life than he had back then. Even when Coby's cancer had drained him, Finley hadn't lost an ounce of love. When Coby died, Finley had too. He just hadn't found himself in the ground yet. Everything he did now felt pointless. There was no chance he would ever find a love that matched theirs. He didn't want to try. Finley couldn't explain why he bothered with Silas and his parties, except Silas' husband, Benji, had run away a couple of months ago and Finley had found himself giving a damn. He hadn't thought he would care about any damn thing again. Now there was the whole Grayson thing. Grayson seemed lonely and anxious. He had a terrible time even meeting Finley's stare for long. Finley couldn't ignore him when it was so painfully obvious everyone had.

Without thinking too much about it, Finley snagged his phone from the dresser. He was already worried about Grayson again. When Finley had left the party, Grayson had been headed upstairs. Finley wondered if he made it.

Finley: *Did you make it to your room safely?*

Grayson: *Yes. Silas made Benji and me some hot chocolate, but they've gone to bed now.*

A smile tugged at Finley's lips. He was glad Silas and Benji were taking care of Grayson, even though he felt like Grayson needed a bit more attention than the occasional hot chocolate.

Finley: *Are you in bed?*

Grayson: *Yes. Are you?*

Finley: *Not yet. I've only been home about five minutes. Did you remember to brush your teeth?*

Grayson: *Oh yeah. I need to do that. I'll be right back.*

Finley stared at the face of his phone and watched a minute tick by.

Grayson: *Okay. Done.*

Finley: *Nope. Try again. That was only a minute. It should've been two.*

Grayson: *Sigh.*

Another smile exploded across Finley's face. He enjoyed himself more than he should. This time, it was three minutes before Grayson texted again.

Grayson: *I'm back.*

Finley: *That's better. Are you all tucked in?*

Grayson: *Yes.*

Finley: *Would you like me to call and read you a bedtime story?*

Grayson: *Please?*

Without hesitation, Finley hit the tiny phone icon and called Grayson. Grayson answered on the first ring.

"Hello?"

Finley could not stop smiling. "Hey, wee one. Let me grab a book."

"Okay."

Damn. He just sounded so sweet and warm. Finley missed cuddling. It took him a minute to find the book he used to read to Coby. The story was an old Scottish tale about swimming amongst the stars. It was soothing and always had Coby asleep four pages in. Finley read. Grayson stayed so silent, he couldn't tell if Grayson was still there any way except checking the timer on the phone. At the end of the story, there was still silence. Finley hated not knowing if his book helped.

"Are you sleeping?"

No response came. Finley disconnected the call. He didn't know if he made any difference in Grayson's life at all, but even if Grayson didn't need him, Finley had a bad feeling he needed Grayson. He was tired of being alone.

Chapter Two

Even though he wasn't completely sure where Finley planned to take him, Grayson dressed with care. The last thing he wanted was to embarrass Finley in public. He pulled out his best soft plaid shorts and polo shirt. Grayson made sure his curls were as tame as possible. He took several deep breaths before heading downstairs where Silas claimed Finley waited.

As he traversed the final steps to the first floor, Grayson caught sight of

Finley waiting by the door. He stood patiently. A V-neck t-shirt showed off a hint of dark red chest hair. The muscles in his forearms looked very thick and lickable. His sexy green gaze swung Grayson's way. The breath caught in the back of Grayson's throat. He was always taken off guard by Finley. Grayson wanted to crawl into his arms and feel safe. He had never wanted anyone like this. Then Finley smiled like he was happy to see Grayson and something inside Grayson melted. He had to win Finley. There was no other option. This was the one he wanted.

"Hey. Are you ready for a fun day?"

Confusion had Grayson's eyebrows drawing together. "I thought we were going to lunch." Which was great, but Grayson didn't see eating as fun.

A smile filled with silent laughter stretched Finley's lips. "We are. That doesn't mean we can't make it an adventure."

Grayson had no idea what that meant, but he let Finley usher him from the house and into his Bentley. As they left the city behind, Grayson's curiosity grew. He hadn't asked a lot of questions before Finley's arrival, since he was just happy to go somewhere. Now he had a million questions, and he was too scared to ask them. He made note of every turn they made, trying to figure out where they were headed. When they pulled into a circular driveway in front of a huge country estate, Grayson looked Finley's way with his eyebrows raised.

Finley didn't leave him guessing. "This is my place. I thought we could eat sandwiches by the pool and then go swimming."

Grayson was torn between over-the-top excited and being realistic. "You didn't tell me to bring swim trunks or anything."

"It's okay." Finley pulled behind the house and into a garage. "I wanted today to be a surprise, so Benji loaned me some swim trunks for you."

Grayson tried not to leap from the car the moment they were parked. He hadn't been swimming in years because it was boring to go alone. Finley opened his door and Grayson climbed out, hoping to look composed. Then Finley led him through a mud room and out a different door. Grayson saw the pool. There were floats and water guns.

Balls and pool noodles. Grayson fought the urge to dance in place. He wanted to jump in.

As if Finley read his mind, he shook his head. "Food first. I don't want you starving later." He motioned for Grayson to sit at a nearby patio table. Once he was seated, Grayson eyed his surroundings. The backyard was so big, Grayson didn't know where it ended. There was also a pool house and a veranda with a built-in grill and refrigerator. Finley grabbed drinks and already made sandwiches from the fridge. He found chips and napkins. It took a couple of trips for him to bring everything to the table. Grayson waited until Finley was seated to unwrap a sandwich. It was ham and cheese, which wasn't his favorite, but it was fine. Grayson just wanted to play in the pool.

"Thank you for lunch. Everything looks good."

Finley opened a bag of chips. "It's no problem. When you're finished with your lunch, I made cookies too."

Unexpectedly, Grayson fought a blush. Finley had gone through a lot of trouble for him. The idea of Finley planning this day around Grayson's happiness made Grayson feel warm all over. Surely Finley's thoughtfulness meant something. Grayson hoped it meant Finley liked him as a little more than friends. That was what Grayson wanted.

The promise of cookies and swimming had Grayson eating faster than usual. They didn't talk through lunch. That was fine with Grayson. Seeing Finley's house reinforced how out of Grayson's league Finley was. He had to keep telling himself Finley wouldn't have invited Grayson if he didn't like him. Grayson only managed that thought because of what a therapist told him once when he had admitted to feeling as if he didn't fit in, even when people chose to be around him. She had told him to force himself to remember no one was obligated to spend time with him. They picked him. He was worthy. Grayson still wasn't sure he believed any of that, but he tried.

When the food disappeared, Finley gathered their trash and nodded toward the pool house. "If you head through that door, you'll find swim trunks on the couch. Go change and I'll grab those cookies."

Grayson stood and took one step toward the pool house before he remembered his manners. "Thank you for everything." He didn't wait to hear a response from Finley. Grayson darted inside the pool house before he embarrassed himself. He didn't want Finley to see the truth in Grayson's expression. Grayson didn't really have friends. He was slightly overwhelmed by Finley.

Inside the pool house, Grayson spotted the swim trunks immediately. They were the perfect size. There was a bathroom within sight. Grayson dipped inside. He quickly changed while trying not to catch sight of himself in the large mirror that covered almost an entire wall. Grayson had a lot of things about himself he didn't like. He always felt imperfect and lacking. The last thing Grayson wanted was to ruin the day by drowning in his own head. With his swim trunks on, his clothes folded, and nothing left to keep him procrastinating, Grayson stepped outside. He nearly swallowed his tongue.

Finley lingered near the table where Grayson left him, but now he wore only black shorts. They were short, showing off thighs that were thick with muscle—like tree trunks. His ass was round and looked squeezable. His torso was covered in hair. Grayson's entire body hummed. He could already picture Finley between his thighs and staring at him while he pumped inside Grayson. Grayson pressed his hand to his stomach. He craved Finley's touch.

Finley's green gaze slid Grayson's way.

Grayson tried to control his breathing.

Finley smiled. "Hey there, wee one. Do you want these cookies now or would you rather swim for a while first?"

Grayson struggled to make his voice work. "Later," he finally croaked. Grayson really loved being called "wee one" by Finley. He felt special.

"I'll leave them in the Ziplock then." Before Grayson thought of a way to respond, Finley closed the distance between them and tossed Grayson into the pool. It happened so fast, Grayson nearly inhaled a gallon of water before coming up sputtering and coughing. Finley roared with laughter before jumping in with him. Grayson wanted to be mad, but flying had been fun, and Finley immediately scooped Grayson into his arms. He clung to Finley's wide shoulders while

Finley carried him into deeper water. The moment they reached the center of the pool, Finley threw Grayson through the air into the deep end. Grayson automatically swam back. His cheeks ached from smiling. They splashed and dunked each other. Finley easily tossed Grayson around. They played for hours. By the time the sun dipped low and the air chilled, Grayson was exhausted. After changing back into his clothes, he ate his cookies, and some cheese-flavored crackers Finley found for him. Grayson fell asleep in the car on the way home. He didn't wake until Finley tucked him into bed.

Grayson didn't want Finley to leave, but he was too tired to fight his heavy eyelids. He would just take a quick nap, and then he would text Finley to thank him for an amazing day. That was the last thought he had before the world disappeared.

For several minutes, Finley watched Grayson sleep. He was the sweetest guy Finley had met in years. Even after spending the entire day together, Finley still didn't know much about Grayson. He was shy and spoke very little. Grayson didn't need to tell Finley a thing. It didn't take a genius to know Grayson had obviously been severely neglected. He was too small for his age to have been stunted from anything other than malnutrition. Finley had watched him eat. Grayson visibly ate at a slow pace, as if he had taught himself to not look desperate. Finley had spent the entire day studying him. He didn't see any signs of physical abuse, such as scarring, or bones set incorrectly. But it was obvious Grayson had been ignored to the point of criminal, and Finley wanted to fix that.

When his presence in Grayson's room bordered on creepy, Finley slipped away. Benji had let them inside and unlocked Grayson's bedroom for him. There was no sign of him now. As much as Finley adored Benji, Finley was grateful to be left with his thoughts. He needed to think. The day had been equal parts amazing and heartbreaking. Finley hadn't played like that since his husband died. He wasn't looking for a relationship or trying to replace Coby, but he couldn't lie to himself either. Finley liked Grayson as more than a friend. He had fought the urge to kiss Grayson all day. Finley had definitely touched Grayson way more than necessary. They had a spark. Finley thought he should probably stay away from Grayson, but he already knew he wouldn't. Grayson had his attention.

Finley drove home on autopilot while his mind churned. The moment he stepped inside his house; the sensation of drowning washed over Finley. He went right back outside. Finley sat at the patio table and stared at the now calm pool. Finley tried forcing his thoughts away from Coby without luck. Coby had been a Little too, but that was where the similarities with Grayson ended. Grayson was quiet and sweet. Coby had been loud and bratty. Passionate. Finley's body ached every time he thought about their life together. He missed being touched.

The final year of Coby's life, they hadn't made love. Coby had been too sick. It was crazy to Finley when he thought about how it had been over two years since he had been with anyone sexually. Time just seemed to pass without his participation. Since moving to New Orleans, Finley only worked part time. He had lost his love of being a doctor when he hadn't been able to save Coby. Finley didn't think he had any real control over anyone's health. He could treat people. Maybe even prolong a life. But Finley had zero ability to save anyone... even himself. He knew he was slowly suffocating alone, but he couldn't imagine ever being intimate with anyone else again. His heart had died with Coby. He didn't want to love anyone else.

Finley's phone buzzed in his pocket, startling him from his spiraling thoughts. He stood and dug the phone from his pocket before reclaiming his seat.

Grayson: *Thank you for today. I'm sorry I fell asleep on you.*

A smile exploded across Finley's face.

Finley: *I had a good time. Thank you for agreeing to spend the day with me.*

Grayson: *Maybe we can do it again sometime.*

Finley: *I'd like that. Get some sleep. I'll text you tomorrow.*

Grayson: *Okay. Goodnight.*

Finley: *Goodnight.*

For several seconds, Finley stared at his phone until the truth hit him. He was smiling at the device like an idiot. Until that moment, he hadn't recognized the truth. He was fucked.

Chapter Three

In the two weeks since Finley had made Grayson lunch and taken him swimming, they had spent nearly every day together. Finley took Grayson on trips to the park, arcades, and museums. He kept Grayson busy. It was nice. Grayson was getting better at talking to Finley. Mostly, they just enjoyed each other's company. Finley still hadn't given Grayson any signs he wanted to be more than friends. Grayson wanted that, though. He needed to know where they stood.

Grayson craved kisses and cuddles, but Finley never did more than offer the occasional hug. Sometimes, though, Finley would look at him in a certain way that made butterflies stir in Grayson's stomach. Those were the moments that gave Grayson hope.

Despite not being very good with words, Grayson knew he had to say what he wanted. Otherwise, nothing would change. He needed to know where things were headed. Grayson didn't want to live in limbo when he could be climbing into Finley's lap whenever he wanted if they were a couple. Since they'd met, Finley had shown at every one of Silas' parties. Tonight was no different. Side by side, they colored in Grayson's favorite coloring book. It was an adult book with lots of curse words. The book was at odds with itself. Just like Grayson.

There were things Grayson liked about being an adult, but mostly, he wanted what he never had: to be cared for and loved. Finley was the first person to make Grayson feel like it could happen.

With his heart in his throat, Grayson scooted closer to Finley, hoping he wouldn't be overheard. He kept his voice low. "Finley."

Sweet green eyes swung his way. "Aye, wee one?"

Grayson licked his lips and swallowed. He had never been more scared in his life. He had a question he needed answered. "Will you be my daddy?" In his nervousness, the words came out in a fast and jumbled mess. Grayson knew Finley understood, though. His expression answered before his mouth said a word.

"I can't do that, angel. My heart belongs to someone else."

It was like getting kicked in the stomach. His eyes burned. Grayson couldn't breathe. As much as he wanted to handle the rejection well, he had to get away. Finley was Grayson's friend, and he didn't want to lose that. But Grayson had also thought they were spending time together for a reason, and they weren't. Without meeting Finley's stare, Grayson shoved his coloring books into his backpack. His hands shook with hurt and anger. He had never put himself out there before. Grayson had honestly thought Finley felt something for him. He was beyond humiliated. Crayons rolled across the floor in his rush.

"Let me help," Finley said, sounding patient. His tone only enraged Grayson more. He was so calm. Finley was always gentle. It made the humiliation worse. Grayson wanted to be wanted, goddamn it.

He snatched the loose crayons from Finley. "I'm big enough to do it."

"Grayson."

Grayson stood, clutching his half-closed backpack to his chest, and leaving some of his crayons behind. If he stayed a second longer, he would cry. He had already embarrassed himself enough for one night.

At the edge of the playpen, a man lifted Grayson over the edge and set him on his feet on the other side. "Hey there, little one. Why are you running away?"

Grayson sniffed. A stuttered breath left him. It was getting less likely by the second that he wouldn't fall apart. "I need to find a daddy."

The dark-haired guy smirked. His brown eyes flashed with wicked intent. "I'm free."

"He's not looking for you," Finley said behind Grayson with that fucking calm-ass tone that was four inches beneath Grayson's skin.

Grayson took several rapid breaths. His chest rose and fell with each one. "I can find my own daddy," Grayson screeched at the top of his lungs, completely losing it. Before he could draw another breath to scream again, Finley plucked him from his feet, leaving Grayson no other choice but to wrap his legs around Finley's waist.

"Someone needs a nap." He pulled Grayson's hood up and then tucked Grayson's face against his neck.

Grayson wanted to punch, kick, and bite. He was angry and hurt. So damn hurt. No one wanted him. He wondered if even his parents had. Grayson couldn't remember. "Put me down." His voice shook with rage.

Finley held him tighter.

Grayson bit Finley's neck in his rage. The moment his teeth sank into Finley's flesh, something shifted in the air. Finley moaned. He coughed to cover the sound, but it was too late. Grayson had heard. Power rose inside Grayson. He wasn't helpless. Grayson could make Finley want him. Finley said his heart belonged to someone else, yet he spent all his time with Grayson. This other person obviously didn't want Finley. Grayson did. He didn't bite hard enough to hurt. His open mouth against the side of Finley's neck turned into Grayson sucking. He treated Finley's neck like a chew toy. Grayson sucked and nibbled. Finley didn't push him away or complain as he carried Grayson upstairs.

At the door, Finley snagged the key clipped to Grayson's backpack and let himself inside. Grayson expected Finley to set him away and leave after the way he behaved downstairs. Plus,

Finley had already said he didn't want Grayson. But when Finley set Grayson on the bed, he came with him. Their mouths met. Grayson's heart soared. The front of his pajamas loosened, and Finley's mouth moved south, kissing the newly bared skin. Grayson lightly gripped Finley's head while gasping for air. He hadn't realized how desperate he was for human touch until Finley gave it to him. Then Finley stilled. His lips skimmed Grayson's chest in the sweetest of kisses. Finley took a stuttered-sounding breath and Grayson felt the moisture on his skin. He realized Finley was silently crying. Grayson's heart shattered. Not for himself, but for Finley. Grayson was always the burden. Finley had been good to him. Grayson didn't want to drag him down.

He hugged Finley. "It's okay."

Finley blew out a sigh and rolled away. He covered his face. "I'm sorry."

Grayson stared at Finley in confusion. He didn't know what he had done wrong, but it was obvious Finley was in genuine pain. "Don't be sorry. It's okay if you want to tell me this was a mistake." Grayson didn't know if that was true. Likely, it would gut him if Finley said those words, but Finley had already told him his heart belonged to someone else. Grayson should have stood his ground after that moment and not let Finley kiss him.

Finley dropped his hands and turned his face Grayson's way. He looked shattered. "I should explain."

"You don't have to." Grayson didn't know why he kept letting Finley off the hook. He just couldn't hear he was a mistake. Grayson was always the mistake.

"My husband died a year ago," Finley said, blanking Grayson's mind. "I'm sorry," Finley repeated, making things worse. "It's not your fault. There's nothing wrong with you. In fact, I like you a lot. I'm just not ready to move on, and I'm not sure I want to be ready. It's not fair to you, but." Finley motioned at himself as if his breakdown should cover any questions Grayson might have.

Grayson was oddly relieved. The problem really wasn't him. Grayson zipped his pajamas. He couldn't do this while exposed. "I understand."

"I should've stayed away from you."

Ouch. "Please stop talking now."

Finley rolled from the bed.

Grayson wished his gaze didn't follow Finley's every move, but he was everything Grayson wanted and would never have. Despite truly understanding Finley's side, he still fought tears. He had let himself dream and hope. Worst of all, Grayson had let himself get attached. He tried hard to be brave. "Thank you for the time you gave me. I'm sorry for everything."

Finley looked ready to growl.

Grayson didn't understand why he aggravated Finley so much. He was the one who had been rejected. Fuck.

Grayson was trying to be an adult and God knew that was not his default setting.

"You told me to stop talking. Maybe you should too."

That was fair. All Grayson did was fuck things up anyhow. He nodded and looked away. Grayson wouldn't watch Finley leave. The inside of his head was already uglier than he could handle. It was best if he never saw Finley again. It was time to let this dream die.

Finley wished he had words. Grayson didn't deserve this. Finley had led him on. They both knew it. Yet Grayson kept apologizing, like everything was his fault. Fuck. Finley wanted to yell at the top of his lungs. Grayson wouldn't look at him any longer and Finley felt the waves of pain rolling off him. It had been a long time since Finley had been this ashamed of himself, but he still left. He walked away. Every step from Grayson's bedroom to his car was hell. He felt like he left the sunshine behind to get back to his empty house.

As Finley walked through the door and his footsteps rang out, reminding him of his loneliness, Finley snapped. His temper completely shattered. He screamed at the top of his lungs. Finley had kept things bottled up for too long. He wanted to be happy. Coby had told him to keep going. He didn't know how.

Finley stormed through the house, searching for something to break. By the time he made it to his bedroom,

Finley deflated. He sat on the edge of the bed and stared at nothing. At some point, Finley had become the bad guy. He let his pain become someone else's. Grayson was just so fucking perfect for Finley. He wasn't playing a role, hoping to snag a sugar daddy. Grayson was just clinging to an identity that hurt the least. Finley knew that without asking. When Grayson didn't know Finley watched him, his every line screamed neglect and loneliness. They matched.

Then Grayson had thrown a fit and bit him. Finley had felt more like himself in that moment than he had since Coby died. He recaptured something when they kissed. Unfortunately, the reality of what he had done hit harder and faster than expected. He felt like he cheated on Coby, and Finley hated himself for that.

Finley sprawled out and stared at the ceiling. He knew Coby was gone. God knew his body felt the neglect. Tonight, for a moment, life had been different. He could still feel Grayson's body beneath his. Finley felt Grayson's desire. It was addicting, feeling alive. Wanted. Grayson was nearly half his age. He should have been joining the party, looking for someone young and sexy for the night. Instead, he had been with Finley.

Finley closed his eyes. The needy and exposed way Grayson had looked at him while asking Finley to be his daddy wouldn't leave Finley's head. He had never felt more torn in his life than he had in that moment. There was nothing standing in the way of Finley having Grayson. Other than himself, that is. When he had unzipped Grayson's pajamas, he had nearly come right then. His body knew what it was missing. He had craved Grayson since the first time their gazes met. Finley's cock stirred. His body burned. The taste of Grayson's sweet lips still lingered on his tongue. He wondered if he had a hickey from Grayson sucking on his neck. The desire to jump back in his car and go to Grayson was real. It was crippling. Before Finley realized it happened, his pants were open, and he massaged his dick.

Every second Finley had spent with Grayson played through his mind. In that moment, Coby was gone. There was no one but Grayson. He was too turned on to feel guilty. The way Grayson always looked at him had Finley hotter than he could recall being in a long time. He wanted to see Grayson on his knees. Finley pictured it now. He pumped faster, wishing he could come on Grayson's face. Finley knew without going down that road, Grayson would do whatever Finley asked and Finley would give him everything for it.

The tension wound tighter faster than expected. It had been too long since he had let himself enjoy anything. Finley didn't fight it. He pumped as fast as he could. His muscles tensed as he strained to reach release. When his orgasm hit, a cry tore from Finley's lips. He gasped for air as cum coated his shirt. He muscles gave out. His chest heaved as he stared at the ceiling. He couldn't see Grayson again. Finley wanted him too much. There was no guilt in the aftermath of the fantasy of Grayson. That was the final straw for Finley. He could love

Grayson. Finley couldn't let that happen. He wasn't ready.

Chapter Four

Three weeks passed without a word shared between them. Finley swore he felt every second tick by. While he hadn't known Grayson for very long, he had brought a bit of color back into Finley's life. Now things were gray again. Finley hated it. He felt suffocated by the grief he couldn't release. The faithfulness to his long-gone husband had kept him warm at night once. Now that small comfort was gone. His loyalty had become a millstone, dragging him down and away from all happiness. He didn't know what to do with himself. Finley stopped himself from texting Grayson a dozen times a day. There was no peace anymore.

The doorbell rang as Finley pulled his phone out for the sixth time that morning, determined to apologize to Grayson. Finley rushed to the door, hoping against hope it would be him. Benji stood on the other side. A bright smile exploded across his face. He genuinely loved Benji. When Benji had left his husband, Silas, and Finley had taken him in for a few weeks, Finley had found happiness for the first time in a long time. Then Benji had gone back home, taking the smiles with him. That had been the beginning of the end for Finley. Now he wanted things again. It wasn't fair.

"Hey," Benji said, sounding breathless. "I've come to visit."

Finley's gaze automatically moved to the driveway, looking for Silas. He knew Silas wouldn't let Benji out of his sight for long, and Benji didn't drive. Benji's bodyguard, Kage, sat in a black Hummer, waiting. Finley's gaze moved back to Benji. "I'm always happy to see you." He stepped back to let Benji inside.

"I can't stay long. Really, I only came by to give you this." He passed Finley a brightly colored gift bag.

Finley glanced down at the bag as he accepted it. "What's this? It's not my birthday."

"It's from Grayson."

Finley's smile slipped away. "Oh." He wondered if he should hand it back. Finley didn't deserve gifts from Grayson and accepting might give the wrong impression.

Benji startled. "Oh yeah. There's a note." He pulled an envelope from his back pocket and passed it along. "Grayson said you need to read the note first or you'll be confused by the gift."

With a nod, Finley set the gift bag aside and opened the envelope. Grayson's handwriting was gorgeous. It was like he had practiced writing the letter for days. With his heart in his throat, Finley forced himself to focus and read.

Finley,

Growing up, I used to make these for my parents. They were a smaller version, but I'll get to that. Anyhow, my parents died when I was little, and I used to think about all the things they missed. So I made these tiny boxes and put report cards, drawings, and projects school forced us to make for Mother's Day and Father's Day inside. Then I would take them to the cemetery and place them in their tomb with them. It was like I thought they got to be an actual part of my life that way.

Anyhow, it obviously didn't bring them back or anything, but it gave me a way to find peace in a connection I didn't have otherwise. I thought to make a few small boxes for you so you could keep a connection with Coby, but Benji says Coby was cremated. So instead, I made you this. I thought maybe you could keep it close and leave notes for him or whatever. I know this doesn't make up for the position I put you in. There's no way I can give back the kiss you feel I stole from him, but I can do this.

Thank you for being my friend, even if it wasn't for long. It meant more than you know.

Gray

Finley refolded the note and opened the gift. It was a wooden box, but not just any wooden box. The piece was hand carved and beautiful. Coby's name had been burned into the wood with a talent Finley couldn't believe. The box had been sanded and stained in a way that brought out the natural grain. Gold hinges and a clasp completed the piece. Finley was speechless.

Unfortunately, Benji was not. "Grayson told me about the boxes he used to make for his parents, but I had no idea they were so pretty." He leaned in close and inspected the woodwork before backing away again. "They died when he was three," Benji added, proving he hadn't read the note. "Then he went to live with his brother. I think these boxes were the only connection he had with anyone. His brother is pretty famous. He didn't have time for Grayson." Benji lowered his voice as if he didn't want anyone to hear his secret. "In fact, Grayson told me he could remember when he was like four or five, he would push a kitchen chair against the kitchen counter and rummage through the cabinets. He would eat uncooked macaroni noodles because he was starving, and there was no one there to feed him. Who leaves a four-year-old alone for weeks at a time?" Benji shook his head. "It's sad."

Finley had everything and nothing to say at the same time. He had known Grayson had a story, but he honestly hadn't wanted to know it, because Finley knew himself. Finley had known he would feel exactly as he did now: outraged. He needed to act and fix things, but he couldn't hurt Grayson even more than he already had.

Benji moved to the door. "Anyhow, I just came by to deliver your gift and check on you. Oh, and to give you this." Benji dug another envelope from his back pocket.

Finley knew without looking it was an invitation to Silas and Benji's next house party. Each invite looked the same. Without thinking, he set the box aside, closed the distance between them, and accepted the expensive stationery. "Thank you." Even to his ears, Finley's voice sounded gravelly.

Benji kissed his cheek. "I can see you're sad, so I won't stay. You have that want-to-be-alone look about you."

Finley flashed Benji a grateful smile. "I'm sorry I'm not better company."

Benji waved away his apology. "We'll see each other again soon."

With a nod, Finley opened the door and saw Benji out. After a final goodbye, he closed the door behind Benji and returned to inspect the box again. Grayson had put so much care into the piece. Finley didn't deserve it. Grayson had apologized half a dozen times now for something he shouldn't be sorry about. Finley was the bad guy. He shouldn't be receiving gifts from Grayson. Grayson should tell everyone he knew how big of a piece of shit Finley was.

Finley's gaze dropped to the invitation he still held. He needed to see Grayson. It wasn't right or fair, but he missed his blond wee one. Finley traced the letters of Coby's name on the box before flipping open the lid. He placed the letter from Grayson inside.

"Look, Coby. I got a letter from my new friend." Grayson was right. Finley felt a little closer to Coby for no reason at all. It was like a new outlet had been opened for his grief. "I think you'd like him." Finley closed the lid and went back to tracing the letters. "I guess.

Actually, it's possible you'd hate him because I like him a little too much. I kissed him." Finley took a deep breath. "You probably knew that already." Finley drew another breath. "I know you said you wanted me to find someone else to snuggle after you were gone, but I'm not doing too good with it. It seems like a year isn't nearly long enough. Surely you deserved more than that from me." Finley lowered his voice to a whisper, hating that he needed to be completely honest. "I think he needs me, though." He leaned closer to the box and lowered his voice even more. "Did you do this? Did you send me his way?"

Finley blew out a sigh and leaned away. He felt like an idiot. It wasn't as if Coby could answer him. He carried the box to the living room, where Coby's ashes sat on the mantle. He sat the box next to the urn. A folded paper beneath the urn caught Finley's eye. He pried it from beneath the urn and unfolded the coloring book sheet he had forgotten he placed there. The image wasn't what stood out, but the note Coby had written for him in the corner did. "You're irresistible when you smile. Keep doing that shit."

A snort escaped Finley as he put the drawing inside the box Grayson carved for him. "Message received, Brat. I still miss you, though." Finley would miss Coby forever, but maybe it was time to let himself have a little happiness. Grayson needed him. Finley couldn't ignore that. Pretending to be dead hadn't helped him. He wouldn't do that anymore.

Grayson lightly held Hoppy's leash and let the bunny bounce around the backyard. He had never had a pet growing up, so he appreciated Tommy and Kage for letting him watch Hoppy every chance he got. It still scared him a little to be responsible for another life. Grayson wasn't very good at anything. He wasn't always sure he could keep anything alive. Thankfully, he was only watching Hoppy until Kage and Tommy came back from taking Benji to deliver his gift. Grayson tried not to think too much about that. There was a real possibility Finley would throw his present in the trash. Grayson tried to prepare himself for anything.

"Jacob called this morning, looking for you."

Grayson didn't look Silas' way at the news. He didn't want anyone to see how much it hurt, knowing Jacob knew how to get ahold of Silas, but didn't know his own brother's number.

When he didn't respond, Silas pushed on, as if they had a two-way conversation. "He says he'll pick you up Saturday night for dinner at eight."

Grayson nodded, letting Silas know he heard. Jacob wouldn't show. He never showed.

"I told him to meet you around the corner since we're having a party that night. I don't want him thinking he could make the guest list."

A smile tugged at Grayson's lips. He imagined that stung the hell out of Jacob's pride. "I imagine that's why he chose Saturday, hoping he would get an invitation." God knew it wasn't because he wanted to see Grayson. Grayson loved his brother, but that love didn't go both ways. Jacob didn't love anyone. Of course, Grayson would still wait for him, because he was a dumbass who never stopped hoping someone might love him a little someday.

Silas snorted. "No one sneaks into my parties and someone like him has no business here."

It warmed Grayson's chest that he belonged somewhere Jacob didn't. That warmth bled away as quickly as it hit. Grayson wished he fit in everywhere. He wished he wasn't different, and that everyone adored him the way they did Jacob. Sometimes he wondered how much more silence he could take before insanity claimed him.

Kage, Tommy, and Benji joined them in the garden. With a smile, Grayson passed Hoppy's leash to Tommy while Tommy signed his thanks. Grayson fought the urge to immediately ask how things had gone with Finley. He needed to make himself not care. His final apology had been made. There was nothing more he could do to make amends. The apology wasn't about him. He needed to be okay with that.

Benji touched his arm, leaving him no other choice but to meet Benji's stare. His light gray eyes looked sincere.

"He seemed really moved by your gift."

A sad smile pulled at the corners of Grayson's mouth. "I think I'll go take a nap." He couldn't talk about Finley. Grayson had never been good at expressing his feelings.

Benji nodded and let him go. There was a hint of pity in Benji's eyes. Grayson had to get away from it. He would always be that sad charity case. The unwanted orphan. All ties had been cut with Finley now. He needed to be alone.

Chapter Five

Silas Dreco's parties were notorious in certain circles. People outside a specific lifestyle had likely never heard of the man known for using his endless funds for people who lived outside the societal norms. Despite Finley's deep-seated need to be a caretaker, he didn't truly fit in at Silas's. Since that was where Grayson was, Finley pushed aside all discomfort and went. He couldn't take another day without his wee one.

The large stone wall surrounding Silas' property hid a sight to behold. After giving his invitation to the guard at the gate, and having it scanned with a black light, Finley was let inside the courtyard of a beautiful four-story home. Men lingered outside, wearing expensive tuxedos or lavish costumes. Sexy, trim men moved from person to person, serving drinks and flirting for tips. Finley only had one goal: to get inside to Grayson.

The doors stood open, allowing light to flow outside and air to flow in. Finley ascended the steps and weaved through the crowd, making his way to the back corner of the ballroom. That was where an area had been designated as a giant playpen for the Littles. Men in nothing but diapers waited to be collected by men who were into that sort of thing. There were a few men in pajamas. Others were dressed like petulant teens. Everyone had their reasons. Still, Finley was there with one purpose. Unfortunately, he didn't see Grayson. He spotted Benji. Benji noticed him at the same time and met him at the edge of the pen. His light gray eyes flashed with happiness.

"Hey. I didn't think you'd come." Before Finley responded, Benji added, "You're not dressed for the party."

Finley glanced down at his jeans and t-shirt. "Aye. I really only came for Grayson."

A line appeared between Benji's eyebrows. "Grayson isn't here tonight. He had dinner plans with his brother, which was a big deal because he never sees him."

Finley tried not to look disappointed while he nodded. "Okay. Well, I guess I'll head out, then."

"You don't have to go. Since you're already here, you should get a drink or something." He rubbed Finley's arm. "It makes me sad to think of you going back to an empty house."

Benji was sweet to worry about Finley. "It's fine. I'll probably binge-watch a show or something. This really isn't my scene. I'm more of a quiet-night-in type of person."

Benji slowly nodded. "Oh. Okay. I'm still happy to see you."

Something warmed in Finley's chest. He genuinely cared about Benji. Benji was so adorable in his teddy bear pajamas. He was exactly the type to worm his way into Finley's heart. Finley had a soft spot for people untainted by life. Those were the ones who deserved protection. He leaned over the pen's edge and hugged Benji. "I'm always happy to see you too."

After a final squeeze, Finley headed back out. He ignored everyone as he made his way back through the front gate and around the corner to his car. Finley climbed inside with a heavy heart. He had truly hoped to get some time with Grayson. Grayson was under his skin, and Finley missed him. He didn't like the way things had been left. Finley needed to make things right. He wanted Grayson back in his life.

Finley started the car and moved to pull away from the curb when he noticed a familiar head of blond curls in the path of his headlights. Grayson sat alone on a park bench down the street. It was late and dark. Finley couldn't leave Grayson there. Not to mention. Grayson was why Finley had shown tonight in the first place. Finley wouldn't miss his chance to see him. He killed the engine and slipped from the car.

Grayson didn't look his way until Finley stood over him. That was enough to give Finley chills. Grayson was too innocent to even look out for trouble. He was a sitting duck on a park bench in New Orleans. A sad smile touched Grayson's lips before he looked away and took a bite of the sandwich he held.

Finley took that as a silent offer to join him. He filled the spot next to

Grayson. "I thought you were going to dinner with your brother tonight."

Grayson shrugged while he chewed. "We had plans, but he didn't show. I made this sandwich, in case he forgot me, because Jacob always forgets me."

Finley wanted to punch someone. Grayson sounded so accepting. It wasn't right. "Why do you bother with him if he disrespects your time?"

Grayson shrugged again. The gesture alone broke Finley's heart. It was obvious Grayson was so used to being mistreated, he thought it was all he deserved. "He's famous. I don't think I told you that, but that keeps him busy. I mean, I'm just me. I can't expect to be high on his priority list when he has lots of celebrity things to do."

"You're his brother. You should be at the top of his list."

Grayson glanced his way, looking genuinely confused by Finley's claim. "Why? He didn't ask for me. I just landed on him."

Finley wondered if he would pop a vein. "Is that what he tells you?"

Finley took another bite of his sandwich. "I worked it out for myself," he said around the bite. He swallowed before continuing. "I've had a lot of time to think over the years. Jacob was already nearly grown when I was born. There was no way he could've known my parents would get caught up in a ten-car pile-up, leaving him with me. He has a great career. Not many people make it as far as he has. I imagine I was a huge inconvenience."

Grayson stared at nothing. "That's pretty much the story of me, though. No one wants me or wants to want me. That's just life for some people." Before Finley could respond, Grayson looked his way. "You're dressed pretty casual for a Silas' party."

Finley chose to be honest. "I didn't come for the party. I came to see you. When Benji said you were out for the night, I left. I wish I had known you'd been stood up. We could've gotten you some real food."

Grayson glanced at his half-eaten sandwich. "Have you not eaten tonight?"

Finley shook his head. "I came to steal you away for a dinner date."

For a moment, Grayson didn't respond. When he did, his generosity blew Finley away, as always. He held out the uneaten portion of his sandwich. "You can finish this if you'd like. You're bigger than me. It probably takes more food to sustain you."

Finley pushed the sandwich out of the way and claimed Grayson's mouth instead. "Mhmm. Peanut butter."

Grayson chuckled against his lips.

Finley deepened their kiss. He couldn't let Grayson get away. The truth was always staring him in the face. Grayson was amazing. He deserved so much more than life had given him. Finley was in the position to give him everything. He wouldn't keep pushing his luck by keeping Grayson at arm's length. Coby would want him to be happy, and he would definitely want Finley to save Grayson.

Grayson turned his head, ending their kiss. "Sorry. I didn't mean for that to happen. I know it's not what you want."

Finley grabbed Grayson's jaw and pulled him back. "For fuck's sake. Stop apologizing," he mumbled as he recaptured Grayson's lips. Grayson didn't fight him. Now that Finley had decided he would take back his happiness, he couldn't get enough. Anger had him in its grasp too. He couldn't believe the amount of neglect Grayson tolerated from everyone, including him. That ended today. Finley pulled away when his rage made their kiss more aggressive than intended and he nipped Grayson's bottom lip.

He snagged what was left of the sandwich and ate it. While he chewed, he pulled Grayson to his feet. "Let's get some real food. I have some things I need to say."

Grayson allowed Finley to hold his hand as they headed for the car. Finley couldn't stop smiling. Things were definitely looking up.

Grayson was happy, sad, scared, and confused, all rolled up into one. It hurt being stood up by Jacob, as usual. He hadn't expected Finley at all. Then Finley had kissed him, and now they were going to dinner. Grayson didn't have a clue what happened in the last half hour. It seemed like things were changing, but he was too scared to hope. Then Finley held his hand. It was nice, but Grayson didn't want to get attached. Finley had said he couldn't be Grayson's daddy. Grayson had to remember that.

He was so wrapped up in his feelings, he didn't realize how quiet he was being until Finley pointed it out.

"It's okay to talk. I won't bite."

Grayson racked his brain for something to say. Before he figured it out, the truth escaped. "I'm scared to say anything that'll make you take your hand away. You made it pretty clear you don't want me."

Finley pulled into a parking lot and parked, as if this required his full attention. He brought Grayson's hand to his lips and kissed Grayson's knuckles. When his gaze swung

Grayson's way, Grayson nearly sighed. He looked so sweet and steady. Grayson didn't think he could be blamed for wanting Finley.

"I'm sorry for making you feel unwanted. I recognize I should've worked through my feelings before I hurt you. In my defense, since the moment I met you, I've been swept away. It's hard for me to move past losing Coby. But if you're still willing, I want to be with you. There's no doubt in my heart. Meeting you just sideswiped me a bit."

Grayson melted. His night went from terrible to amazing in an instant. Heat filled his cheeks as a smile tugged at his lips. There was no way he could tell Finley no. "Oh. Okay. I'd like that."

Finley leaned his way. Grayson didn't hesitate to close the final gap between them and press his lips to Finley's. It was a sweet kiss. Their lips brushed and clung. Grayson wanted to climb into Finley's lap for cuddles. Between dealing with Finley's rejection for a few weeks and Jacob's latest letdown, Grayson felt overwhelmed and exhausted. He needed his Dino pajamas and to be snuggled. Kisses were amazing. They made his skin tingle, but insecurity still had him in its grasp.

As if Finley felt his neediness, he slid his seat as far back as it would go, unsnapped Grayson's seatbelt, and hauled Grayson across the car into his lap. With Grayson sideways across Finley's thighs, Finley held Grayson tightly against his chest and placed light kisses against the shell of

Grayson's ear. Grayson's entire body relaxed. Air filled his lungs. He unclenched his teeth. Until that moment, Grayson hadn't realized how he had been holding himself together by tensed muscles and nothing more.

"You're worthy of attention and affection. It's not your fault your brother is selfish. That's no reflection of you. In fact, it's his loss because you're absolutely amazing, wee one. He doesn't deserve you and neither do I."

Grayson's eyes stung. It was as if Finley read his mind and plucked out the words Grayson needed to hear the most. Grayson wasn't special. He likely had nothing to offer someone like Finley, but he would try. Grayson planned to give Finley all the affection and keep watch for whatever Finley needed from him. Finley wouldn't regret letting him in. Grayson would be a good boy.

"Let's go in this restaurant and get you something to eat."

Grayson turned his head and glanced toward the building. He hadn't realized they were in the parking lot of a restaurant. It looked fancy. He fidgeted at the idea of sitting in a nice place after the ups and downs of his night.

"Can we get our food to go and go back to your place instead?"

"If you'd like."

Since Grayson heard the laughter in Finley's voice, he pushed his luck.

"Can we go through a drive-thru and get hamburgers and fries?"

"Is that what would make you happy?"

A bright smile lit Grayson's face. He wanted a kid's meal. His favorite place was giving away toy cars this month. "Yes."

Finley kissed his ear again. "Okay, wee one. Get your seatbelt on and tell me where I'm going."

With a giggle that sounded happy even to him, Grayson scrambled back to his seat. He was ready for the heaviness to disappear. Finley offered an outlet. Plus, he really loved tiny hamburgers. Life looked so much brighter.

Chapter Six

With his tongue held between his teeth, Grayson focused completely on drawing a pattern across his fries with ketchup. Finley couldn't look away. Everything about Grayson fascinated him. He felt younger and older at the same time in Grayson's company. That last part truly hit home tonight. Until now, he hadn't worried too much about Grayson's age or anything pertaining to that, because he had been determined they would only be friends. Now they were more, and that age gap kept sneaking into Finley's thoughts.

"I need to ask you something."

Grayson's adorable green eyes shifted from his food to Finley. "Okay."

Finley's stomach muscles clenched with hunger. In fact, he was too hungry. That meant they needed to talk. He felt like a lecher, though. "Um." Finley cleared his throat. "I'm a lot older than you."

Grayson blinked, as if Finley's words confused him. "Okay."

Finley cleared his throat again. "I imagine that means I have a lot more sexual experience than you."

A blush exploded across Grayson's face, but he didn't look away. "Okay. That wouldn't be hard, even if we were the same age."

Damn. That was what Finley figured. Finley nodded his understanding. "That's all I needed to know. You don't have to worry. I would never rush you into anything. We'll go slow until you're ready."

Grayson nodded and ate his fries.

Finley watched with a knot in his gut. He needed to ignore his desire and let Grayson decide when to take the next step. Grayson's happiness and comfort meant more than Finley's needs. After all, Finley hadn't been with anyone in a long time. Surely he could survive spending time with Grayson without falling on him like a lunatic. He had made it this far.

Grayson polished off his fries and drink. He stood. "Okay. I'm ready."

It was Finley's turn to blink. Surely Grayson didn't mean he was ready, ready. Finley needed clarification. "For what?"

"To have sex."

Grayson wasn't blushing now.

Finley didn't want to seem as if he planned to turn him down, but he had expected Grayson would want to move slower. "Are you sure?"

Grayson nodded. "I was ready when you carried me to bed a few weeks ago. This is better, though."

Finley imagined so, since he wasn't crying this time. He spun his stool sideways and motioned Grayson closer. The moment he was within snagging distance, Finley pulled Grayson between his knees so Grayson couldn't get away. "I'm sorry if I ever made you feel unwanted." He ran his hands down Grayson's back and cupped his ass. "You're very sexy and very much wanted."

A shy-looking smile touched Grayson's lips. "You are too."

Finley drew Grayson closer. "You can tell me to stop at any point and I will."

Grayson nodded. "Okay. Stop."

Finley immediately dropped his hands. "Fair enough."

"That was just a test," Grayson said, snagging Finley's shirt. He hauled him down for a kiss. "We're not stopping," Grayson said as he claimed Finley's mouth.

Finley exploded into action. While still exploring Grayson's mouth, he came to his feet and lifted Grayson from his feet by his ass. He left Grayson no other choice but to wrap his legs around Finley's waist. Finley headed down the hall. He was on fire. Finley hoped he could keep his word about going slow. He didn't want to hurt Grayson. It was Finley's job to keep him safe and baby him.

The moment they reached the bed, Finley found himself on his back with Grayson undressing him. At some point, the control had flipped, and Finley didn't want it back. Grayson had things in hand... literally, setting Finley free from the worries he had about hurting Grayson. When they were both shirtless, Grayson settled down on Finley's chest and snuggled against him. He ran his fingers through Finley's chest hair.

"Oh. Oooh. This is nice."

Finley wondered if his brain would snap under the pressure of his lust. Grayson felt pretty nice in his arms, though.

A heartbeat passed and Grayson licked his nipple. Finley bit back a moan. Grayson did it again. Finley broke. In a flash, he had Grayson flipped onto his back. Finley tore at the remainder of his clothes, barely sparing a glance for the cartoon-themed underwear Grayson wore. Nothing mattered but the man beneath the clothes. Not even that. Nothing mattered except connecting as deeply as he could with the person who had found him at the darkest point in his life and saved him. That was the real reason Finley needed to be as close as he could get to Grayson. Grayson had saved him and given Finley life again. Finley wanted to make Grayson soar.

In a matter of seconds, Finley had his lips wrapped around Grayson's cock. A whimper caressed Finley's ears as he took Grayson down his throat. Finley licked and sucked while using his wet fingers to probe and stretch Grayson's asshole. He didn't know if Grayson was ready for him.

Wishful thinking had him diving for an old bottle of lube that was buried deep in his nightstand. He was back with lubed fingers before Grayson had time to beg. Finley needed to spend some time prepping Grayson. Grayson was way too tight. Finley was scared Grayson wouldn't come back if Finley hurt him too much. He needed to make Grayson feel good.

Grayson squirmed beneath Finley as Finley bobbed on Grayson's cock while massaging his prostate. Tiny mewling sounds filled the room. Finley's entire focus was on pleasuring Grayson, even while his body begged for the same treatment. Grayson's body tensed. Finley braced to swallow. Instead of the flood of cum he expected, Grayson grabbed Finley's hair, pulled, and twisted. Once again, Finley found himself on his back. This time, Grayson straddled his body and impaled himself on Finley's dick.

"No." The cry escaped Finley even as his body sang. "Baby, I'm not wearing a condom." At odds with himself and his claim, Finley held Grayson tightly against him.

Grayson stared down at him with a lust-filled gaze. His eyes looked unfocused, and his lips were swollen from their kisses and Grayson biting them. "I'm sorry. I thought you only wanted me."

Finley's heart twisted at the hurt in Grayson's voice. "Of course, I only want you, but I also want to keep you safe."

"What are you keeping me safe from if you only want me?"

Goddamn. He was so innocent, and Finley had no response with Grayson's tight asshole sucking him deeper. When he didn't respond, Grayson wiggled a little on Finley's dick, as if he couldn't stay still.

"Daddy, I need..."

Finley knew how to make it better. He rolled, pinning Grayson beneath him. "I've got you, wee one."

With his knees buried in the mattress, Finley held Grayson in place and gently rocked inside him. While ensuring he hit at the perfect angle, Finley massaged Grayson's cock.

Grayson scratched at the covers beneath him. "Please. I... please."

Finley understood. He would fix it. Finley couldn't pound inside Grayson the way he wanted. This was all too new to Grayson. So Finley kept his thrusts shallow and slow. He felt Grayson's muscles tense again. Finley saw stars as Grayson's asshole clamped around his cock.

"Aye, wee one. That's it. You're so close. You feel so good. I'm proud of you. You can do this. Show Daddy how you can come. I want to watch."

Cum shot from Grayson. A tiny cry caressed Finley's ears while Finley worked every drop from Grayson. Grayson's body tried sucking Finley deeper. Finley ground his back teeth so hard, he expected something to crack. He clasped Grayson's hips so tightly, his fingers left indents on Grayson's skin. The pressure in his balls nearly crippled him. Then the air whooshed from his lungs as the first spasm hit. A cry tore from his throat.

He rocked, pumping Grayson's ass full of cum. His little angel would be leaking the rest of the night. Finley couldn't wait to care for him. He would keep Grayson clean and warm. They would cuddle and kiss. If Grayson felt like it, maybe Finley could show him even more ways to make love. There was nothing but hope inside Finley. They were perfect.

Inside Finley's hold, Grayson felt warm and safe. His body hummed in the aftermath of their lovemaking. He wanted to be embarrassed by some aspects of the aftereffects, but Finley wouldn't let him. Finley kept cleaning him and praising him, as if his body's betrayal was beautiful and part of the experience.

Every time Grayson wondered if Finley had fallen asleep, he would kiss Grayson's temple again. Grayson couldn't stop smiling or petting Finley. He had never been this happy, or this terrified. Before now, Grayson really hadn't had anything to lose. Now he wondered if he would survive if Finley never spoke to him again. He was hyper aware Finley could shut him out now. There was nothing tying Finley to him. It was possible sex was enough for him. Grayson wasn't important. He had nothing to offer.

"You should start a website and sell your boxes online." Finley's claim came from nowhere and took Grayson off guard.

"What?"

"That wooden box you made me," Finley clarified. "You should sell them. You're amazingly talented. People could benefit from your gift."

Grayson blushed and hid his face.

Finley didn't let it go. "I'm serious. People love handmade gifts, but they're not as readily available these days. I'm not saying you have to buy a workshop and spend all day sanding, but you could bring people comfort and happiness."

"It's just a hobby." As much as Grayson appreciated Finley's praise, he didn't think he was as good as Finley made him out to be.

Finley rubbed his arm. "I won't pressure you. It's just something to think about."

Before he realized it would happen, Grayson confessed his fears. "I worried you would think the box was stupid. It's just something I did as a kid. I was always alone, so I used to steal scraps of wood from one of the crumbling hotels taken out by Katrina. It was just something to keep me busy."

"So, no one taught you how to do any of that?"

Grayson shook his head. "I had a lot of free time."

"Damn, wee one. That's impressive. Most people take classes and work for years to get as good as you are."

Even though Grayson understood Finley was just being nice, he appreciated the compliment. "It's nothing the least bit useful, but it's all I have."

Finley shifted positions so he could meet Grayson's stare. "You have me. Not only that, but you have the best heart and the sweetest smile. You have a thousand things to offer this world. I'm lucky as hell you choose to waste your time with me."

Finley was a doctor and well respected. It was humbling to hear praise from him. Grayson didn't know if he would ever believe a word of it, but that wasn't Finley's fault. He wouldn't belittle Finley's words by denying them. Instead, he went with a different truth. "You make me happier than I've ever been. I want to be the same for you, but I can't promise you won't be completely disappointed."

Finley rolled, pinning Grayson beneath him and cuddling him hard. He kissed Grayson several times in a row, until Grayson couldn't stop laughing.

"Stop talking like that."

"I was just being honest."

Finley kissed him repeatedly again until Grayson laughed too hard to speak. "I'm serious. If you keep talking like that, we'll do this all day. You're mine now. You're not allowed to insult yourself."

Grayson could have kept playing all night, but Finley's nude body was between his thighs. He was highly aware of the way their bodies molded, and Finley's weight pressed against him in the most delicious way.

Grayson squirmed a little. Finley's cock stirred. Grayson's laughter died. Finley lowered his head and their kiss turned serious. All thought disappeared. Grayson was a mess. Likely that wouldn't change. He had been neglected past the point of abuse and life had left a scar he couldn't remove. Finley's kiss didn't feel like he was bothered by that, but Grayson didn't doubt it would eventually be an issue. For now, though, he would take as much happiness as he could get. Finley was absolutely amazing. Grayson wanted more.

Chapter Seven

Finley: *I have one more patient to see today and then I'll be free. What would you like to do when I get home?*

Grayson: *Can we go swimming again?*

Finley: *Of course.*

Grayson: *I'm watching Tommy and Kage's bunny while they're out of town this*

week. Is it okay if I bring her over? If not, you could stay with me.

Finley: *Whatever we need to do so I can see you is fine with me.*

Grayson: *Yay!*

———— *ele* ————

Grayson: *I sold two boxes online today!!*

Finley: *I knew you could do it. You're amazing.*

———— *ele* ————

Finley: *I'm leaving the office in ten minutes. What's the plan?*

Grayson: *Can we go shopping? I feel very accomplished making extra money now. Let's spend it.*

Finley: *Whatever makes you happy, wee one.*

Grayson: *You make me happy.*

Finley: *Same.*

Spending time with Grayson was no hardship. In fact, they spent every free minute together. He made Finley feel fifteen years younger. Even though Grayson wanted to spend his money, it was Finley's job to care for him. Every store they visited, Finley paid before Grayson could until they got to the last one. At the mall, Grayson darted inside a toy store and bought a huge bear before Finley could protest. He handed the bear to Finley with a shy smile.

"It's for you."

Finley kissed the bear's nose. "He's perfect."

When Grayson smiled, looking proud, Finley herded him toward the car. He didn't have any arms left to carry things.

By the time they made it back home, Finley was exhausted. They had eaten dinner, bought Grayson a new one-piece dinosaur costume and three new Lego sets, and dropped Grayson's latest finished orders by the post office.

Finley sank onto the couch with a bottle of water and focused on Grayson while Grayson stripped. His exhaustion disappeared as each new inch of skin was bared. Sometimes, he thought he was too old and tired for

Grayson. Then Grayson would look at him in just a certain way, and Finley was over it. Grayson was his. Finley wouldn't give him up.

Grayson pulled on his new costume and zipped up the front. His smile spoke volumes. As long as Grayson was happy, Finley was too.

"There's a sexy dinosaur. I like your tail." The outfit had a thick tail lined with soft spikes. The hood had teeth that nearly swallowed Grayson's smiling face. "Roar," Grayson said, sounding adorable while fake clawing at Finley's knees. "I'm speaking to you in dinosaur language. Roar means I love you."

Finley's smile slipped away. It was instant. He hadn't expected that. Grayson's claim caught Finley off guard. He didn't return the words. Finley couldn't. His throat swelled. Being with Grayson was one thing. Loving him was another. Finley wasn't prepared. He didn't know what to say or how to react.

A flash of something dark passed over Grayson's features when Finley sat frozen. He didn't doubt his expression said everything. Finley would not be saying the words back. Grayson turned away and sat on the floor. He dragged his shopping bags closer and tore into a box of Legos. In his head, Finley turned over every second they had spent together, looking for any signs he had misled Grayson.

Finley definitely had a type. He always found himself drawn to Littles because it was a power relationship. He loved to be the caretaker, but he was also the one in charge. Coby had been a huge brat. But when Finley had enough of his mouth, he would turn Coby over his knee and spank him into submission. In Coby's case, Coby had fallen back on being a bratty Little because he had recognized it gave him a certain seductiveness that drew men to him. He had been incredibly sexy. Preening, pouting, stamping his feet, and then cuddling afterward had been how he always got his way. Grayson was different. He regressed into a Little to find joy and when he needed to protect his heart from a life that had done nothing but kick him at every turn.

Fuck. Finley was the bad guy. He just kept hurting Grayson every chance he got. Finley didn't know how to stop. It wasn't as if they were moving too fast. Grayson was completely within his rights to expect their relationship would progress into exchanging words of love. But at every new milestone, Finley fought him. He didn't know why he did these things to Grayson. Finley knew he wasn't being fair. He was so trapped in his fear that Finley didn't realize Grayson stared at nothing like he was lost in thought. His Legos sat ignored. Grayson's stillness choked Finley. Finley swore he could hear Grayson's thoughts churning. When Grayson shifted to his knees at Finley's feet, Finley's throat swelled. He knew Grayson had decided. Grayson was done with Finley now. Tonight had been too much crap for even him. He would leave Finley alone to suffer in his bullshit by himself the way he deserved.

"Can we have hot chocolate, Daddy?"

Finley's chest squeezed and relaxed so fast, he wondered if his heart would stop. The relief was that massive. Grayson wasn't leaving. Finley recognized two things simultaneously. It would kill him if he lost Grayson, and he absolutely loved Grayson too. He was also heartbroken because he realized Grayson hadn't been playing with his Legos hurt over Finley not returning his words. He hadn't expected Finley to say it back. Grayson didn't expect anyone would ever love him, but Finley did.

"I love you, wee one. Do you want marshmallows too?"

Grayson nodded. His hood bobbed along with his head. A smile exploded across Finley's face. He hadn't expected to be this happy again. It was all due to Grayson. Before he could push to his feet to make Grayson's hot chocolate, Grayson set his hands on Finley's thighs, stopping him. He looked more serious than usual. His gaze didn't waver from Finley's.

"I changed my mind."

"Okay." Finley was slightly confused, but whatever made Grayson happy was fine with him.

"You've been busy doing things for me all night. I haven't gotten to do anything for you."

"That's not true. You bought me a bear."

Grayson shook his head. "That's not good enough. You deserve more." His hands slid higher, and he shuffled closer between Finley's knees. "I want to know I give you more." Without warning, Grayson dropped his face and moved his head from side to side while roaring loudly so that it looked like a dinosaur was eating at Finley's crotch.

A laugh burst from Finley. His stomach ached with it as Grayson's playing turned more ridiculous by the second. Realization washed over Finley as he hauled Grayson into his lap. Grayson gave him so much more than he knew. Happiness and laughter hadn't existed before him. It would leave if he did. Finley wanted to know that wouldn't happen.

Finley wrapped his arms around his squishy Dino. "Do you really want to give me something?"

Grayson nodded against Finley's neck.

"Move your things in," Finley said before he could change his mind. "Let's get your stuff from Silas's so I can take care of you full time. If you want to give me something, give me you."

Grayson was so still in his arms, Finley wondered if he was about to get shut down. Instead, a light kiss brushed his neck and a soft *rawr* purred against his skin. "That was Dino for yes."

Finley couldn't stop smiling. It had been the best night. He couldn't wait for a million more.

The last four months with Finley had been the greatest of Grayson's life. He didn't know why Finley wanted to keep him, but Grayson was in. In fact, he was bursting with happiness. No one had ever wanted him around as far as Grayson could recall, and Finley had said he loved Grayson. His heart was full. Grayson needed to know Finley wouldn't regret keeping him.

After nuzzling Finley's neck, Grayson slipped from Finley's arms and back to the floor. Without an ounce of hesitation, he went straight for the button on Finley's pants. Finley's sexy, light green gaze followed Grayson's every move, as if curious to see how far Grayson would go. Grayson would go to any length to keep Finley. He was still pretty new to learning all the ways to please a man, but Grayson was willing. Grayson liked it when he made Finley moan.

As he slid Finley's zipper down, the bulge in Finley's underwear moved.

Grayson felt powerful. He saw the way eyes followed Finley everywhere he went. Grayson understood he owned a prize. When Finley spoke and people heard his accent, their eyes lit, stirring all of Grayson's jealousy. But Grayson wasn't helpless because he knew Finley's body. He knew what Finley liked. Finley was a huge guy who could toss Grayson around like a toy. But Grayson knew how to bring him to his knees.

His body tingled with anticipation as he set Finley's erection free. Finley was so pretty and cuddly. He made Grayson ache with a constant need to be closer. As Grayson lowered his head, Finley swept Grayson's hood away, as if he couldn't stand anything blocking his view. Grayson ran his tongue up Finley's cock. A stuttered breath fell from Finley's lips. The sound had Grayson fighting the urge to stroke himself. He opened his mouth over Finley's crown and lightly sucked.

Grayson hadn't learned the trick to swallowing Finley's dick without choking yet. He liked to try, even though Finley said it didn't matter. Before he could give it a shot, Finley pulled him away. He shifted forward and kept coming until Grayson was on his back on the living room floor, with Finley hovering over him. Finley's eyes burned with emotion. Grayson couldn't look away. No one had ever stared at him the way Finley did, as if he was special. He was Finley's sole focus. It was addictive.

"You make me burn."

"Good." Honestly, Grayson didn't want to sound obnoxious, but he needed Finley to crave him.

"It's not enough to make love to you. I cannae sleep without you anymore. You're all that exists in my head."

Grayson sucked in a deep breath. He knew when Finley's Scottish accent thickened, he was about to get fucked. They had passed the point of Finley making love to him. Nothing sweet came next. "I want to be all you think about for the rest of your life." They were the truest words Grayson ever spoke.

"Done." With his vow still hanging between them, Finley's mouth covered Grayson's. They fought to get closer. The one-piece costume easily parted beneath Finley's practiced fingers. While Finley's tongue filled his mouth and roughly played with Grayson's tongue, Finley held their erections together and thrust. Grayson saw stars and clawed Finley's skin. He swore Finley had a new move every time they had sex. It was like he tried teaching Grayson all the different ways they could find pleasure together. Finley had done nothing Grayson didn't like yet. He wanted all of it. Every trick Finley could throw his way, Grayson craved more.

He quickly found Finley's rhythm and matched it. They strained together, but Grayson wasn't sure if their orgasm was the only goal they hoped to reach. Every thrust felt like it went emotionally deeper. They were cementing something real. This was the first night of a new life. Tears rolled back into Grayson's hair as reality washed over him. Finley had fully chosen him. They would be together forever. He had a home with this man. Grayson had never felt this full.

Chapter Eight

Grayson was on top of the world. He couldn't put into words how it felt to have Finley come home to him every night. It was a life he never expected to have. There was a kid inside of him that had bigger dreams, though. He still wanted his brother to be part of his life. Christmas was around the corner. The night Grayson moved in, Finley had bought them a tree, and they had decorated it together. Then Grayson had gotten this idea. He would invite Jacob to dinner to celebrate the holiday. There was one major obstacle in the way of that plan. Once again, Jacob wasn't answering his calls.

He wanted to give Jacob his new address and tell him everything. Grayson knew he could text Jacob, but honestly, Jacob never responded to Grayson's texts. He didn't know if Jacob even got them. So, with his heart in his throat, Grayson headed for Jacob's front door. He wasn't sure if Jacob was there or if he would answer. Grayson was more than a little worried about a million things. Technically, Jacob didn't know Grayson was gay. Jacob knew nothing about Grayson. He had been so busy with his career, he hadn't noticed anything about Grayson. Grayson wasn't sure how Jacob would react. He comforted himself that Finley was a doctor, so maybe that would look good on the boyfriend resume for Jacob.

After several minutes of knocking and ringing the doorbell, the door finally swung wide. A taller and buffer version of Grayson stared out at Grayson. "Oh. Gray. What's up?"

Grayson smiled. "Hi. Is it okay if I visit for a minute? I have news."

Jacob looked a bit strained as he glanced at the expensive watch on his wrist. "Yeah. It's cool. I've got like fifteen before I need to head out."

Grayson's knees unexpectedly shook as he stepped inside the home where he had spent most his life. It was huge and meant for a star. Grayson hated the place. There were no good memories here. He didn't know why he couldn't stop reaching for Jacob. Nothing good ever came from it.

Jacob spoke over his shoulder as he headed for the kitchen. "I've been meaning to stop by and see you. It must be amazing living with Silas Dreco. You should be proud." Jacob picked up a half-empty cup of coffee from the marble counter and took a sip. "That's one powerful friend you've made. I've been trying to land an invitation to one of his private events for years. No one has ever told me what goes on there, but anything that coveted has to be awesome."

Grayson decided to gloss over the whole party thing. People didn't talk about Silas' events for a reason. They were a bit no see no tell when speaking with people outside the lifestyle. Jacob was straight as an arrow. He did not want that invite. However, there was no time like the present to jump into the reason he was there. "Yeah. My living situation is kind of why I stopped by."

Jacob's eyebrows rose. "No."

Grayson put his hands behind his back to hide the way they shook. "No, what?"

"No. You can't move back in." Jacob set his cup aside. "We've had this discussion. You're nineteen now."

"Twenty," Grayson said, even though Jacob wasn't listening.

"If I coddle you, you'll never make it in this world. This world doesn't give a fuck about your feelings. You need to man up and find a way to support yourself. Do you even have a job?"

Grayson thought to tell Jacob about his website and the boxes he had been making. He couldn't. Grayson didn't want to be mocked. "Sort of."

"Sort of," Jacob repeated with a snort. "See? That's what I'm talking about. You somehow managed to weasel your way into living with the Silas Dreco, but now you've fucked it up. Do you have any idea how far you could go if you took advantage of his connections? Instead, you're here, looking for another handout. You're weak."

"I'm not looking for a handout." Grayson's voice shook, but he didn't stop. "I came for my brother. Christmas is around the corner, and I wanted to invite you to dinner at my new place so you can meet Finley."

Jacob's face screwed up in confusion. "Finley? Who in the fuck is Finley?"

Grayson swallowed. "My boyfriend."

Jacob's features snapped closed. "What did you just say to me?"

"My boyfriend." Even to Grayson's ears, he sounded small.

A cruel smile with no humor spread across Jacob's face. "I know you didn't just tell me that you not only fucked up having a connection with one of the most powerful men in New Orleans but you're also gay. Do you realize everything you do reflects on me?" He took a step closer. "Do you understand that if you land on the cover of a gossip magazine that it's because you're fucking up my reputation?" He grabbed the front of Grayson's shirt and hauled him closer until they were nose to nose. "Do you know what people will say about me?"

Too late, Grayson smelled the alcohol on Jacob's breath. His insides shook with fear. He already knew there was no right answer in this situation. It was already too late for him to turn back. There was no escape.

With his final patient seen and his notes sent for the day, Finley gathered his things to go home. Home. Damn. He finally felt like he had one of those again since Grayson came to live with him. Grayson had only been there a week, and Finley already felt whole.

He had their future all planned out in his head. Every day, he let joy win a little more. He felt better than he had in years.

Finley headed for the parking lot. He had a stop he wanted to make on the way home. When they had moved Grayson's things from Silas's, workers had been at Silas' place building an adult-sized jungle gym in the backyard. Now that Finley had the idea in his head, he wanted to surprise Grayson with one too. He was excited to see what the company had to offer. Maybe he would also get a tree house built. The possibilities were endless.

As Finley slid behind the wheel of his car, his phone rang. A smile pulled at the corners of his mouth when he saw Benji's name. Between Benji rekindling his marriage and Finley falling in love with Grayson, they didn't talk as much as they should. He missed his friend.

Finley started the car before answering the call so the Bluetooth would connect, and he could talk while he drove. "Hello?"

"Where are you right now?"

Finley's smile fell. His brow furrowed. "I'm leaving the office. Why?"

"You need to head to the hospital. Something's happened."

Finley's heart sped. "Are you okay? Did something happen to Silas?"

"It's Grayson."

Finley's heart stopped for half a beat. "What about Grayson?"

"He went to see his brother to tell him about you. It didn't end well. I don't know how bad it is yet, but you need to get here. The nurse I just spoke to said he's been moved to critical care, and that's all they could tell me."

Finley's fingers went numb. "Okay. Yeah. I'm on my way." He didn't know how his voice still worked. Everything felt surreal and way too familiar. He had been leaving work when Coby had been moved to critical care. Finley hadn't made it in time to say goodbye. He couldn't do this twice in one lifetime.

Finley put the car in gear. The hospital was down the street from his office. It wouldn't take him long to get there.

His foot wouldn't lift from the brake. Reality kept him frozen. He wasn't meant to be happy. If ever the universe saw him smile too much, he lost the object of his happiness. That meant this was on him. His bad luck had captured Grayson and made him pay for loving Finley. The only way to save Grayson was to stay away. Maybe no one else would understand the insane way Finley immediately jumped to that decision, but Finley knew the truth. He was cursed. Loving Grayson had doomed him. Finley's heart couldn't take it. Something Benji asked him once came back to haunt him. He asked how Finley would feel if he knew Coby was alive and happy somewhere in the world, but would never be with Finley again. Finley had answered honestly. He could live with anything if Coby could be alive and happy. Finley could live with anything as long as Grayson was alive and happy. Grayson's brother had done this awful thing because of Finley. Finley couldn't live with that. If Grayson didn't make it, that was on Finley. He needed to know Grayson was alive and happy. Otherwise, there was nothing good left in the world. Finley killed the engine and sat in silence while he tried making his thoughts less insane. They wouldn't budge. He was caught in an endless loop of doomed scenarios. Unless someone had brought home the ashes of the person they loved the most in the world, they wouldn't understand. No one else could understand what it was like knowing his husband's body burned until there was nothing left but ash. He would never see Coby again. Coby would never laugh or smile. If Grayson died, Finley couldn't know it. He couldn't do another round of screaming at the top of his lungs for someone who would never exist again. Finley wasn't strong enough. When Grayson needed him the most, Finley couldn't deliver. His cracks showed. He couldn't be there for this.

Chapter Nine

Not for the first time in Grayson's life, his heart hurt so bad, he thought he might die. He slept for almost a week, squished between Benji and Silas until he stirred enough from his stupor to realize they probably wanted some time alone. Still, without them, he wouldn't have eaten or drank, much less taken his meds. Grayson didn't care about anything anymore. The world had finally broken him. His brother despised him enough to try to kill him. Finley had fallen off the map.

Then his things had arrived from Finley's house via messenger. Finley hadn't even bothered to bring them himself. Grayson had nothing left. He had disabled his website and canceled the last of his orders. It wasn't like he could carve boxes with only one working hand.

Grayson was slowly regaining sight in his left eye, but his right arm was broken. He had three ribs that would likely never be the same and pneumonia had set in not long after his lung had been punctured and collapsed. Grayson was tired, and it had nothing to do with the pain medication that made life tolerable by keeping him asleep. He simply didn't want to keep doing this breathing thing any longer. Every heartbeat hurt. It took almost a month and lots of prodding from Silas, but Grayson was dressed and on his way to face Finley. He knew it was a waste of time. They were as done as two people could be, but Finley would look him in the eyes and tell him why. As Silas had reminded him a million times, Grayson deserved that much. Maybe then he could move on, but he doubted it. Grayson didn't think there was anything to move on to.

Benji's personal bodyguard, Kage, drove in silence. He kept tossing worried looks Grayson's way. Grayson got it. He was more bruise than he was skin, even with nearly a month to heal. Grayson looked as dead as he felt. He didn't care anymore. Grayson had no fight left in him. As the circular drive came into view that led to the house Grayson thought he would share with Finley, he fought a flinch.

He closed his eyes and took a shallow breath.

"Do you want me to go with you?"

Grayson's eyes opened. He forced a small smile to his lips. "No. Thank you. I appreciate the offer, but I'm humiliated enough."

A dark scowl touched Kage's features. "You have no reason to feel that way. He's the one who should be embarrassed. No real man abandons his man at the hospital."

The fact that Kage knew his story only made the humiliation thing worse. Grayson's entire life had been humbling. He was ready to stop now. There shouldn't be any lessons left to teach him. "Nonetheless."

Kage gave him a sharp nod, letting it go. "I'll be waiting."

With a dip of his chin to acknowledge Kage's words, Grayson slipped from the SUV. The front door opened before Grayson made it up the steps. His eyes burned at the sight of his cuddly bear. Grayson almost melted to the ground. He wanted to rush into Finley's arms. Finley's closed expression stopped any ideas he had about trying. It hurt so much worse than he could have ever dreamed.

"Benji told me you were on your way and not to make you walk up the steps." Finley moved from the doorway to sit on the top step.

Grayson stopped at the bottom of the steps. His heart ached so much, he didn't doubt it showed in his eyes.

"Why?" He didn't say more. His voice wouldn't let him. But Grayson didn't think he needed to clarify, since they both knew why he was there.

"I'm sorry for the way things ended, but I just can't."

Grayson needed more than that. "You just can't what?"

Finley openly eyed Grayson's injuries and then scrubbed at his face. "Any of this. After watching Coby die, I just don't have what it takes to get left behind again. I can't do this. I'm not strong enough to risk my heart again. I thought I could, but I just can't."

Grayson nodded. He understood this part. Grayson had been here his whole life. Completely unwanted. "That's fair. I got left behind when my parents died, so I get it. I understand not risking your heart again. But for the record, I also know that means you never really loved me."

Finley jerked, as if Grayson slapped him.

Grayson didn't stop. "You're almost twice my age, and I know—realistically—that means you'll likely die before me, but that still didn't stop me from loving you. If you can stop yourself from loving me, then you never did."

"It's not that I don't love you."

"It is," Grayson said, cutting him off. A sad smile pulled at the corners of Grayson's mouth. It hurt his face. "I should know. No one has ever loved me. I know exactly what it feels like when it's happening. It feels just like this."

"Grayson, I—"

Grayson walked away. He might not be able to make anyone love him, but Jacob had finally taught him one lesson. Grayson knew now he shouldn't keep trying.

Finley had always been great at hating himself. Still, as he watched Grayson walk away, he hit a new low. It wasn't that he didn't recognize that he had completely self-destructed the first moment he thought he might get hurt. Finley one hundred percent knew that. But Finley hadn't truly accepted how cruel his decision had been. He wanted to chase after Grayson, but not only did he not deserve forgiveness, Finley knew Grayson was better off without him. But fuck if he didn't miss him. Finley had never wanted to hold and comfort someone so badly in all his life. He had lost that right.

Despite knowing Grayson deserved better than him, Finley couldn't let Grayson go completely. He dug out his phone and texted Benji.

Finley: *Grayson just left.*

Benji: *That's sad. I hoped you would take one look at him, fall to your knees, and beg forgiveness. You really were such a cute couple.*

Finley: *He deserves someone younger and less fucked up. With that said, is there any way you can send all his bills my way? I want to take care of him.*

It took Benji a few minutes to answer. Finley watched three dots jump on his phone, showing Benji typing, and he knew he was about to get told everything he deserved to hear. Finley sat still and waited. It was the least of his penance.

Benji: *I don't know. When I left Silas, it hurt a lot that he thought his money could make up for anything. I mean, I don't mind sneaking you his medical bills, but don't think that makes up for what you've done. Grayson threw all his toys and pajamas away. He disabled his website and is looking into jobs. You broke everything beautiful and unique about him and I would be remiss if I didn't tell you you're bad for that. It was your job to keep him safe. Silas and I trusted you with him. Now he feels wrong for being the person you claimed to love. You know what? You're right. He deserves better than you and I'm mad too. I used to feel very different from everyone, so I've been in Grayson's shoes. You were supposed to be his daddy. You failed him.*

Finley's throat swelled as he read Benji's words. He knew it was all true. Finley had failed. That was the truth of the entire situation. He was supposed to keep Grayson safe, and he hadn't been there to do so. Just like with Coby, Finley had been a complete failure when it counted the most, and it was too much. Without thinking, Finley's fingers moved across the phone. He found himself admitting the darkest thoughts in his head.

Finley: *That's what I do. I fail people. I couldn't save Coby from dying and I wasn't there when Grayson needed me. I don't know how to fix anything because I'm useless when things get tough. Grayson thinks I never loved him, and I did that. He's the perfect one. I'm the mess. He shouldn't have looked my way. I have no business trying to take care of anyone. I can't even take care of myself, so tell me what I'm supposed to do because I don't know anymore.*

The three dots jumped and then stopped. Finley growled and fought the urge to chuck his phone across the yard. Everyone was done with him, and he didn't blame them, but fuck. Too much had happened to him in the last year and a half. He was broken. Just as Grayson had begun putting him back together, Grayson had almost died too. It was no one's fault Finley couldn't stop punishing himself for his inability to save Coby. He wished... he didn't know what he wished. That wasn't true. Grayson knew exactly what he wanted, and it wasn't fair. He wanted his snuggly Grayson back. He wished for a second chance. Finley wanted to prove he wasn't the piece of shit he had turned into since Coby died. His phone dinged, saving him from a complete meltdown now that truth hobbled him.

Benji: *Do you love him?*

Finley: *Yes.*

Benji: *Do you want him back?*

Finley: *Yes.*

Benji: *Then I'll help you make it happen.*

A tear slid down Finley's cheek, and he swiped it away. He had barely been holding himself together for a while.

Now he let himself admit the truth: he had been stupid and wrong. The pain came next. His heart shattered. He had really let fear beat him and his sweet wee one had paid the price. Finley might never get to hold Grayson again. He drew a stuttered breath and another tear fell. Finley wouldn't survive this life without Grayson, and he didn't know if he could make it right. He was an idiot.

Chapter Ten

Silas and Benji's property was surrounded by a tall stone wall. Finley was a big guy who wasn't built for scaling unscalable fences. But there was no length too far for him to go to get to Grayson. Finley measured the exact feet of the fence, starting from the left back corner until he reached the spot Benji had told him to climb. He jumped and snagged the edge of the wall before hauling himself upward. It took several minutes and a long leap of faith, but he managed to hit the spot where Benji had disabled a camera. He only had a ten-minute window before Benji would reactivate the security for that corner of the yard. Benji couldn't and wouldn't risk their party guests' safety for longer than that.

While sticking to the planned route, Finley high-tailed it through the backyard until he reached the house. From there, it was only a matter of acting casual and joining the crowd. Also, he needed to avoid running into anyone who might recognize him before he found Grayson.

Even though Benji claimed Grayson had thrown away his toys and whatnot, Benji had also promised he would get Grayson to the playpen tonight. Finley didn't waste any time. He didn't know how long he could stay before getting busted for party crashing, so he headed straight for the back corner of the ballroom where the Littles played. Finley spotted Grayson immediately. Despite being in the playpen area, Grayson wasn't dressed like everyone else. He wore jeans and a t-shirt. Finley's chest hurt. Grayson looked miserable. He kept his broken arm against his body, as if keeping it safe, while the other men crawled around him, trying to get him to play. As Finley moved closer, he spotted Silas sitting nearby, playing with Benji. His steps faltered, but he didn't stop. Even when Silas' chin lifted and his lips parted in surprise, Finley didn't hesitate to jump the wall of the pen to get to Grayson. Grayson barely spared him a glance when Finley sat beside him.

"Hey, wee one."

Grayson scooted away.

Finley moved with him. "Is it okay if I talk to you?"

Grayson scooted away again.

Finley followed. "Why aren't you wearing your dinosaur costume?"

"I'm too big for that."

Finley fought the urge to rub his chest in an attempt at soothing his heart. "I miss you."

Grayson stood and walked to the edge of the playpen, where Kage waited. Kage stared at Finley with cold eyes, as if daring him to make a move. He lifted Grayson up and over the edge of the playpen before setting him on his feet on the other side. Benji's lawyer,

Max, materialized from nowhere. He put his arm around Grayson and steered him away. Frustration roiled in Finley's gut. He knew he didn't deserve Grayson's time, but he was fucking furious. Grayson shouldn't have given up on the things he loved because of someone like Finley. Finley wasn't worth that. He hated himself and Jacob and everyone else. No one deserved happiness as much as Grayson and the entire world needed to burn for making Grayson feel like he was unlovable as himself. Finley was enraged and had nowhere to go with it. He didn't know how to fix anything.

Silas scooted closer, pulling Finley from his inner meltdown. "I've never had anyone gate crash at one of my parties. You'll have to tell me how you did it, so I can make sure it never happens again."

Finley fought not to look Benji's way and give away Benji's part in things. "I'm very good."

Silas didn't as much as blink. Finley expected he would get tossed from the house now. "Well, you've seen the damage you've caused. What do you plan to do next?"

Rage seethed beneath his skin. Most of it was directed at himself, but it had no outlet. Not only would Grayson never forgive him, which was fair, Grayson was no longer living his truth. All the happiness was gone from his beautiful wee one. While it was mostly Finley's fault, Jacob had a huge hand in things too. He needed to pay.

Finley clenched his fists, causing his knuckles to pop. "I want to beat the shit out of Jacob."

Silas nodded, as if he understood Finley's need for payback. "I've already made sure he was held without bail, so he won't see the outside of a cell for a long time for what he did to Grayson. He was also let go from his sitcom and he'll never work again, if I have anything to say about it, and I do."

"Not good enough." Even Finley heard the seething in his voice.

Without looking Benji's way, Silas spoke to his husband. "Benji, go find Max and stay with Grayson and him until I get back."

To Finley's surprise, Benji didn't argue. He stood, and Kage lifted him up and over the pen.

Silas moved to his feet. "Kage, are you in?"

A cruel smile twisted Kage's lips. "Absolutely."

Silas nodded, and they headed out. There was no going back now. Finley had nothing left to lose. Jacob needed to pay. Finley planned to collect.

———— *ele* ————

Max pushed Grayson on the swing of Benji's new jungle gym. He was gentle since Grayson could only hold on with one hand, but it didn't matter. Grayson couldn't feel anything anymore. He had gone numb at the sight of Finley. Grayson honestly thought he would never see Finley again. Silas had assured him Finley would no longer be welcomed at any of his events. Every time Grayson thought he couldn't be gutted again, life found a new way.

His arm ached tonight, and he wanted to go to bed. Then again, he couldn't go back to his empty room. He hadn't wanted to come to tonight's party, but there was nothing to do in his room since he had thrown away all his toys. Then he had gotten downstairs and still he sat with the Littles because he didn't know anyone or fit in. It had been hard to resist coloring and playing with the blocks, but it was time for him to leave all that behind. Being a weak baby had cost him everything. Grayson had nothing left to give.

"Do you want to talk about it?"

Grayson shook his head.

Max filled the swing beside him. "Do you want to get fucked up instead?"

A smile snapped to Grayson's lips. He wasn't used to people treating him as an adult. "I'm not twenty-one yet."

A sexy-sounding snort escaped Max. "First off, I'm from England. The drinking age isn't the same there. Second," Max pulled a bag of pills from inside his jacket pocket, "you don't have to be twenty-one to do drugs. That's illegal for everyone equally in this state."

Grayson had never been offered drugs. It was actually a bit funny. School had made it seem as if people would offer him drugs on every corner, but this was new. The bag had several different-colored pills inside. Grayson's interest was caught. He liked bright colors. "What are those?"

Max shook the bag and peered inside. "A little of everything. Uppers. Downers. Something to make you happy. Others will make you sleep."

"Is there anything that'll make me not care?"

A bright smile lit Max's face. "I've got you." He dug three pills from the bag and passed them Grayson's way. "Take these at the same time. You won't care about anything for at least twelve hours."

Benji appeared around the corner.

Grayson froze, feeling like a naughty child busted doing something wrong.

Benji glanced between them. "Oh. Are we getting fucked up?" He pulled a bottle of wine from inside his teddy bear pajamas. "If so, I have wine."

A smile exploded across Grayson's face. He accepted the wine to wash down the pills before passing the bottle to Max. They each took turns drinking. Benji chose a blue pill to go with his wine—like they were pairing desserts.

"I do believe I might be the bad influence," Max said after swallowing his pills.

Grayson's head already spun. "That makes you the best of all of us in my book." He set his swing into motion.

Grayson liked the way the cool air felt against his skin. He didn't go too fast so he wouldn't fall, but everything felt faster with the drugs and alcohol mixing in his empty stomach. He couldn't recall the last time he had eaten anything. There came a point when he no longer cared. He almost hoped he would just wither away.

"It's true," Benji said, keeping the conversation going about Max. "I've seen the way men fight for your company. Is that because you do all the bad things?"

A dark and naughty-sounding laugh rumbled from Max. "Not at all. It's because I do some bad things really, really well. In fact," he leveled a stare at Grayson, "I could make you forget the Scotsman. Just tell me all your kinks and I'll bring mine too. It could be one hell of a night. You'll never look at any other man again."

Grayson took another drink of the wine before responding. "I think I might be boring. If I have kinks, I don't know what they are."

"Mhmm, a blank slate. Love it."

Grayson blushed at the naughtiness in Max's voice.

Benji looked thoughtful. "What are your kinks, Max? I like learning new things."

Max shook his head. "Nope. You're married to Silas. He might have me killed if he learns I soiled his baby's ears."

A sweet smile touched Benji's features. "I'm married to Silas. There's no kink I haven't tried."

Grayson was fascinated. No one ever spoke like this in front of him. He wanted to know more. "Like what?" Even Grayson heard the embarrassed curiosity in his voice. He felt wrong, but he also really wanted to know.

To his surprise, Benji jumped right in. "Well, there's the obvious one: age play. Dominance and bondage. Impact play. Role play. Also, I have a bit of a thing for Klismaphilia."

"Oh, Klismaphilia. That's hot."

"What's that?" Grayson whispered the question. He couldn't help it. It seemed wrong somehow to have this conversation.

"Getting turned on by being given enemas."

Grayson nodded at Max's explanation and then motioned for Benji to continue. "What else?"

Benji looked thoughtful. "Object play, electro stimulation."

"Oh, do you two have any tentacle toys?"

At Max's question, Benji seemed scandalized. "Of course. No collection is complete without that and a bit of knotting."

Grayson felt wide-eyed. He had no idea so much went on in other people's bedrooms. Meanwhile, he had just been trying not to gag on Finley's cock.

"It's no wonder Finley couldn't love me. I've never heard of more than half this stuff."

Max scoffed. "Innocence is fucking sexy too. Don't listen to that voice in your head."

Benji looked sympathetic. "Sweetie, Finley fell head over heels for you. That's why he's so dumb. Boys are stupid when they're in love."

"It's true," Max agreed, taking Grayson by surprise. "Men in love are the dumbest creatures alive, and humans are complicated. Things we don't understand scare us and turn us on. We run when we should fight. We stay quiet when we should speak. We fight when we should listen. Life is hard work. I don't know what this guy did and I'm not excusing it, especially if he's the reason your arm is in a cast, but yeah. Boys are stupid. If Benji says this guy loves you, though, I'd believe him. Benji knows everything. He won Silas."

A bright smile lit Benji's face at the compliment, and Grayson couldn't fault Max's logic. Silas seemed to be the ultimate prize. That didn't mean he believed Finley loved him.

"I see both of your points, but I don't think Finley could hurt me the way he did if he loves me."

Both men winced.

"Oh, sweetie," Benji said at the same time as Max said, "That's who we hurt the most."

Grayson was high as fuck, and he felt like this had been the most enlightening night of his life. He didn't want it to end. "What do the blue pills do?"

Benji and Max both smiled like mischievous kids, but Max was the one who responded. "Oh, you're about to have a great night."

Grayson was in. He needed a great night. Things had been shit for longer than he ever dreamed. Bring on the pills. Grayson needed the release.

Finley's split knuckles stung, but his fury hadn't abated. He half expected to get dumped outside the gate of Silas' expensive home after their little trip across town, but Kage drove into the garage, and they headed inside together—as if Finley belonged.

He followed on Kage's and Silas' heels as they weaved through the party. Kage broke away when he spotted his husband, Tommy. Silas led Finley out a set of French doors and around the outside of the house until they reached the new jungle gym. Benji was on his stomach in one swing with his arms extended, soaring like a superhero through the air. Max laughed as he sent Benji flying higher. Grayson was on the ground with his legs on the swing, rocking it back and forth while he stared at the sky.

"Good lord. What did we miss?" Silas asked, taking the words straight from Finley's mouth.

"I took the blue pill," Grayson yelled at the top of his lungs as if he had gone deaf.

Silas plucked Benji from the swing and headed for the house. Benji was already trying to undress Silas before they made it inside.

Finley didn't really know Max. He only knew of him because of Benji. Max met Finley's gaze and dipped his chin before heading inside to rejoin the party. Once they were alone, Finley moved to stand over Grayson. He was wide-eyed and visibly high. His gaze moved over Finley almost frantically.

"There's blood on your shirt."

"It isn't mine."

Grayson nodded. "Why are you spinning, then?"

With a sigh, Finley plucked Grayson from the ground. "If I had to guess, it's because you took the blue pill."

"I took the blue pill," Grayson repeated, as if Finley hadn't just said as much.

Finley made his way through the crowd and up the stairs. When he reached the third floor, he headed for Grayson's room. "Where's your key, wee one?"

"Don't call me that. I'm not a wee one."

Finley's throat swelled. "Where's your key?"

"I lost it the other day. It's unlocked."

Grayson needed a keeper, whether or not he liked it. Finley opened the door. Grayson's bedroom was completely transformed from the last time Finley had been there. All the toys were missing. The brightly colored wall stickers were gone. The room looked as adult as could be. Finley honestly didn't understand. He carried Grayson to bed.

"Why did you get rid of all your stuff?"

Grayson held still while Finley undressed him. His eyes looked unfocused. "I'm not a wee one. Everyone is embarrassed by me. No one will ever love me if I can't grow up. I mean, I can't even suck dick properly, much less get into any sort of tentacle klisma-whatever."

Finley's eyebrows rose. "First off, I beg to differ on the dick-sucking thing, but that's not really important to me anyhow. Second, what in the hell have you been doing while we were apart?"

Grayson's eyes filled with tears. "Hurting." His confession came out in a whisper, shattering what was left of Finley's heart. "Everything hurts. Everyone hurts me." Grayson's eyes fell closed, as if he had a hard time staying awake. "When I woke up in the hospital, it hit me. My big brother— the only family I have—is so ashamed of me, he wants me dead. Then you abandoned me because I was too weak to defend myself." Grayson's voice turned softer by the second. Unchecked tears ran down Finley's face. "So, I won't be little anymore," Grayson whispered. "Maybe one of you will want me again."

Finley's hands dropped. His energy left him. The pain was too much. Even after everything Jacob and he had done, Grayson still wanted them. Finley didn't know how to fix this. He didn't know how to save Grayson, but he had to find a way. Finley couldn't let Grayson stay on this path of loving people who hurt him. He deserved better. Finley would give it to him. No matter what it took, Finley would fix what he broke. He loved Grayson too much to stop now. Finley just needed a little help. Luckily, he knew just who to ask.

Chapter Eleven

For reasons Grayson didn't understand, Silas and Benji were having a party two nights in a row. He imagined they were doing a second night because Benji and Silas had missed last night's party after their wine and pill-popping session. Grayson kind of resented it, though. He didn't think he could handle another night of being a grownup. His head still pounded from the first night. It didn't help that he clearly recalled Finley undressing him for bed. But when he had woken up this morning, there was no sign of Finley. He hated how badly he wanted to pretend nothing happened so he could go back to being Finley's wee one. Life was rarely fair, though. Grayson was well aware of that.

The party downstairs had been raging for more than an hour while Grayson paced inside his bedroom. He knew how many steps the bed was from the door and how many from the door to the bathroom. Boredom set in, driving him half mad. After two hours, he gave in and headed downstairs. The crowd seemed much thinner tonight until Grayson reached the ballroom. That was where the place came to life. The throng was so thick, he had to shove his way through the crowd to get to the playpen. Even though he fully intended to give up playing with toys and wearing baby clothes, he didn't know what else to do with himself during these events.

When Grayson reached the edge of the playpen, he froze. Finley was inside wearing nothing but a diaper. He ignored the huge flock of men vying for his attention, but it was definitely him. Grayson would know that gorgeous hairy body anywhere. Kage touched his arm, pulling Grayson's focus away from Finley. He motioned toward the playpen, silently asking if Grayson wanted inside.

Grayson nodded.

Kage helped him over the edge.

When Grayson's feet touched the floor on the other side, Finley's chin lifted from the blocks he stacked, and their gazes collided. Neither of them looked away. Grayson's feet carried him closer. He didn't stop until he sat across the stacked blocks from Finley.

"What are you doing?"

Finley shrugged. "Proving I'm not ashamed."

His answer did nothing to clear Grayson's confusion. "What?"

Grayson stacked another block on top of his already tall wall. "You said you wouldn't be little anymore, so I won't be a daddy."

Grayson felt the line between his eyebrows getting deeper. "But... what?"

"If you want to change, then I will too. I want to be with you, and if swapping roles is what it takes, then that's what I'll do." He lowered his voice for only Grayson to hear. "I wasn't expecting this much interest in a hairy baby."

Grayson's lips twitched. Finley did not look like a baby. He looked like a daddy in a diaper. Grayson had a feeling that was what drew so much interest. "You did this for me?"

Finley nodded. "I know you can't make someone love you by giving them more of something they already don't appreciate. You weren't the weak one. I was. You deserve someone stronger than me, so I am renouncing my daddy status. I don't deserve it or you. I didn't appreciate you while I had the chance, so I won't be a daddy anymore. I'll find a way to be someone you can love."

Grayson was beyond moved and he couldn't even articulate why. Mostly, he saw Finley fighting for him. That was something he couldn't ignore. "I don't change diapers."

Finley didn't smile like he hoped. "I'm nearly twice your age. We might be at that stage someday."

Grayson nodded, taking the conversation seriously. "We can circle back to the discussion when that day comes."

A sexy smile touched Finley's lips. "What are your thoughts on sponge baths?"

"Giving them?"

Finley shook his head. "Receiving them."

Grayson's smile turned shy. His skin felt more comfortable by the second. "Can I have bubbles?"

"Will you wear your footed pajamas afterward?"

Grayson's smile fell. "I threw them all away."

Finley bit his bottom lip. He looked guilty. "I might've bought you new ones, just in case."

Grayson fought the happiness growing inside him. He hadn't forgotten Finley's abandonment, but he wasn't unmoved. "I can't get my cast wet and long sleeves don't fit very well over it."

Finley's eyes screamed his understanding. "Maybe we can circle back to the pjs after you get your cast removed. The bubbles are no problem with the proper precautions."

Grayson rearranged Finley's blocks. "What should we do in the meantime?"

Finley held his stare. "Maybe we could play for a little while and then you could spend the night at my house."

Grayson nodded. "Maybe so."

Finley didn't rush him. Grayson appreciated that more than he could say. Finley found more toys and together they played. Grayson didn't know how much he was ready to forgive or if they would ever be the same, but he wasn't ready to give up yet. He loved Finley. That wasn't as easy for him to turn his back on as it was for others. He understood how precious and rare love was. Grayson wasn't ready to live without it.

For years, Max had been a regular guest at Silas' parties. Then his twin brother had died, and Max had stopped coming. Without any admissions of guilt, Max knew in his heart Silas was the reason Max's brother was gone, but then again, David had killed himself, really. He had become so obsessive and abusive by the end that Max wasn't surprised he had come to a bad end. Still, Max's anger and hurt had kept him away from these events for a while. Then, one day, he realized he only punished himself. The love of David's life lived here and worked at these parties. Hanging on to Tommy was a way of hanging on to David. Unfortunately, the more parties he attended; the more Max returned to his old ways. He drank, smoked, and took all the pills. Max didn't sleep any longer thanks to all the coke. He imagined he would go the way of David soon. Even knowing didn't save him. Life bored the fuck out of him. Max no longer functioned normally.

He had enjoyed himself more last night while hanging out with the Littles than he had in years. Now he just felt maudlin. Woebegone. Nothing held his interest anymore. He wanted to feel whatever he had felt last night, but with sex. It was like friendship, but he wanted friendship and the dirty stuff. He didn't know what he needed, but life was missing a certain je ne sais quoi. Max wandered outside to the swings and sat. He rocked back and forth without lifting his feet from the ground. His gaze found the stars. Every second that ticked by, his mood worsened. He felt a presence behind him, but he didn't turn to look. Nothing appealed to him tonight. He probably shouldn't have taken the yellow pill... or the red one before that.

"I have a bigger swing in my bedroom. One built for better activities."

A shiver ran down Max's spine at the gruff voice behind him. Warmth engulfed him. The scent of orange chocolates—an expensive cologne that was one of his favorites—surrounded him.

"I also have a milking machine and fucking machine."

Okay. Max was a little less bored. He still didn't turn to look. Max didn't care about appearances. He liked them small and big. Short and tall. Older and younger. Tops and bottoms. Max fucked them all.

Hands gripped the chains of the swing and lifted Max backward until warm breath brushed the shell of his ear. "I also have vise grips and a thousand other fun toys. I could make you bleed... and scream."

Max took a ragged-sounding breath. "I'm in."

A sexy and terrifying chuckle rumbled against his skin. "Good boy."

With two deadly-sounding words from a stranger, Max knew he had found trouble. It was just what he needed to keep going.

Even though Finley never expected to get so much attention with his grand scheme, he refused to feel an ounce of humiliation for doing whatever it took to win Grayson. He had spent his entire life trying to do what was right. Since he met Grayson, Finley had made every dumb choice possible. He didn't deserve Grayson. Grayson should be with someone who treasured his every breath. That person was Finley, and he would prove it.

As Finley watched Grayson walk back through the door of his home, Finley's heart twisted. Without thinking, he immediately swept Grayson from his feet and carried him the rest of the way inside while being careful of his healing ribs. He was ridiculously in love and wanted to care for Grayson, as he should have done from day one. Finley had missed his chance to take care of Grayson in the hospital. He had thrown away the opportunity to dote upon him when he came home. Finley needed to do those things now.

"How do you feel about having that bubble bath? I can keep your arm dry."

Grayson visibly tried to hide his excitement. "Will you take one with me?"

"Of course." Finley carried Grayson to the couch. "Sit here and I'll get it started." He rushed to the bathroom inside his bedroom. That was the only bathroom with a tub big enough for two. Even though he recognized he had driven, and Grayson wouldn't likely leave while his back was turned,

Finley still hurried through starting the water and finding Grayson's bubbles where he had stashed them out of sight. It was almost funny when he thought about it now. He could have thrown the bubble bath away, but he had stashed it deep under the sink, as if he had known he would eventually cave and beg Grayson to come back.

With the tub full, he made his way back to the living room. He found Grayson at the mantel, eyeing Coby's urn. Finley hovered in the doorway. Grayson opened and closed the box he had carved for Finley, as if needing a reason to linger at Coby's side.

"Hi, Coby."

Finley covered his mouth. Grayson sounded so sweet and shy. It hit Finley all over again how much he had nearly lost. He fully understood how dumb his reaction to Grayson getting hurt seemed to everyone else. But people wouldn't understand unless they had been there. Finley couldn't put two urns on his mantel. Loving someone was hard when you knew how much living without them cost.

While Finley looked on, Grayson leaned closer to the urn and lowered his voice. "Is it okay if I keep your daddy? I promise I'll take good care of him."

Finley's throat swelled. He stepped out of sight and made his footsteps known, so Grayson wouldn't be startled or embarrassed by his return. This time, when he stepped back into view, Grayson stood in the center of the living room, looking innocent.

"Are you ready for your bath?"

With a nod, Grayson crossed the room. Hand in hand, they headed down the hall. Inside the bathroom, Finley undressed Grayson. He did his best to hide his rage as he caught sight of Grayson's injuries again. The fury never left him. Even though it had been nearly a month, the marks weren't all gone. He would have a scar forever where they had re-inflated his lung. Finley ground his back teeth so hard, his jaw popped.

"Are you ever going to tell me about your busted knuckles?"

Finley really didn't want to do that. He wasn't sure how angry Grayson would be. Finley helped Grayson into the tub before stripping and joining him. He slipped in behind Grayson so Grayson could relax against his chest.

A contented-sounding sigh caressed Finley's ears as Grayson settled against his chest. A few minutes of silence passed where they simply snuggled in the tub. Finley kept Grayson's arm draped over the edge of the tub so it would stay dry.

"It's okay."

Confusion had Finley's brow furrowing. "What's okay?"

"Benji says the jail guards claimed Jacob was attacked by unknown jail mates. With his jaw wired shut, Jacob can't claim otherwise. Not that anyone would believe him anyhow."

Finley struggled for something to say. He hadn't wanted Grayson to know about his little visit to the jail where Jacob had been held since his attack on Grayson. Without Silas' connections, Finley never would have gotten to the bastard. Likely, Jacob would do some prison time. Unfortunately, in the state of Louisiana, who knew if he would face any substantial consequences. An attack on his brother for being gay just might get some sympathy from backwoods judges. It took Finley a few minutes to find the words to express his side of things.

"I needed him to know what waits for him if he ever comes near you again."

Grayson didn't respond.

Finley couldn't stay quiet. "I know he's your brother, but you have to let him go."

When Grayson still didn't respond, Finley wanted to scream. Finley was overjoyed Grayson possessed a forgiving heart. Otherwise, he never would have won Grayson back, but fuck. He couldn't risk Jacob weaseling his way back in. Finley's heart couldn't take knowing Grayson might forgive him. Before he could figure out how to word his argument, Grayson made a soft grunting sound, the one he always made in his sleep. Laughter gathered in Finley's throat. He swallowed it down. Grayson hadn't been staying stubbornly silent. He was sound asleep.

With a huge smile stretching his lips, Finley used his foot to release the water. When it was low enough that he knew Grayson wouldn't drown, he heaved himself out of the tub and found a huge fluffy towel for Grayson. It took some doing, but he managed to carry a half-asleep Grayson to bed. He tucked Grayson in and then plodded around the house nude, making sure the doors were locked, the alarm was set, and all the lights were turned out.

When he crawled into bed beside Grayson, Grayson rolled into his arms. His hand immediately found Finley's cock. Finley tried to ignore it. Grayson wasn't really awake. The last thing he wanted was to get turned on with no outlet right at bedtime.

Grayson didn't stop. His arm being in a cast didn't hinder the use of his hand at all. Finley took slow breaths, trying to calm his quickly heating blood. When he realized there was no going back, he tried to hyper-focus on each brush of Grayson's fingers, hoping to come quick before Grayson stopped. Then Grayson dipped beneath the covers. His hot mouth sucked Finley's crown. Finley thought his eyes would roll back in his head. He couldn't believe Grayson had worried he didn't please Finley. He drove Finley fucking wild. Finley didn't need some guy who got into things, deep throating and gagging. Grayson had this light suckle and lick that had Finley moaning in no time. It was maddening and sexy. He had to struggle toward orgasm, but when it hit... goddamn. It punched so hard, his entire body shook and cries bounced from the walls. Then Grayson always kept going, like he had only sucked Finley off to drink his cum. Grayson was irreplaceable. There was no one hotter.

The moment Finley regained his senses, he had Grayson on his back. Grayson's dick sawed in and out of Finley's mouth. He needed Grayson to fly. Grayson made adorable mewling sounds while his feet moved restlessly against the mattress. Finley didn't hold back. He sucked Grayson's balls and swallowed his cock. He went wild on Grayson's dick. Grayson's muscles tensed. Finley held Grayson in place so he wouldn't hurt himself when he came. A sexy whimper burst from Grayson as cum flooded Finley's mouth.

Tears hit from nowhere. Finley pressed his face against Grayson's stomach while sobs rocked his body. He had almost lost his wee one. The terror had crippled him. He hadn't been the man he always wanted to be when the chips were down.

Grayson stroked Finley's hair and shushed him. Finley climbed up his body and buried his face in the crook of Grayson's neck. He did his best not to press any weight on Grayson, but he had to hold his precious baby. Finley would never forget or forgive his failures.

"I'm so sorry. I love you. You're my everything. I never should've hurt you. I don't deserve you."

Grayson kept petting him. "I love you too. It's okay."

Finley shook his head. "It's not. I was just so scared. You can't risk yourself like that again. My heart can't take it. I love you. Please don't put yourself in danger again. Please stay away from Jacob. I'll be your family. I swear you won't need anyone else. Please just don't leave me."

Grayson kissed the shell of Finley's ear. "Don't worry. I'm not going anywhere. You're my sweet daddy. I don't need anything else. I love you."

Finley's muscles relaxed a hair at Grayson's words. Then his resolve set in. He had Grayson back under his roof and in his bed. Finley would keep him safe. They would be happy, and Grayson would stay healthy. It was as simple as that. If, for any reason, Jacob came around again, Finley would kill him. Problem solved. No harm would come to his baby. Grayson would see. Life would be beautiful. He would never hurt again. Finley snuggled as close as he could without hurting Grayson. This was forever. Finley would make it great.

Chapter Twelve

Even though they were back to living together, Finley and Grayson still attended every one of Silas' events. Not only did they enjoy the freedom of the gatherings, Silas and Benji were their friends. Grayson liked seeing them. Finley never left Grayson's side during the parties. No one else got Finley's attention. Grayson felt more secure than he had in years. Still, there was something more he needed.

"Daddy?"

Finley looked up from the Legos he was putting together for Grayson. "Yes, angel?"

"Will you push me on the swings?" Finley was having a jungle gym built as an early Valentine's gift at their house, but he enjoyed taking advantage of Benji's play area when he could.

"Aye. Let's go."

Grayson scrambled to his feet and skipped to the edge of the playpen. Finley lifted him over the edge before following him. Hand in hand, they headed outside. There was a bit of a nip to the air, but his pajamas kept him toasty. Outside, Grayson ran to the nearest swing and climbed on. While Finley pushed, Grayson kicked his feet. Still, he didn't find the joy he hoped to find. He needed to fix things.

Grayson dragged his feet, stopping the swing. He turned, twisting the chains so he would spin when he lifted his feet. Grayson toed the ground, trying to work up the nerve to ask something that had been bothering him since he had moved back to where he belonged.

"What's eating you, baby?"

A smile tugged at the corners of Grayson's mouth. Finley knew him too well. Grayson took a quick breath. "Why don't you call me your wee one anymore? Are you still mad at me?"

A deep line appeared between Finley's eyebrows. "I have never, not one time, been angry with you. You asked me not to call you wee one any longer. There's nothing I wouldn't do to keep you, so I've kept my word not to call you that."

"Oh." Grayson lifted his feet and let the swing unwind. He still wasn't happy. There was just this insecurity that never left since their split. He wanted to get past it. Finley wasn't doing anything to make him feel that way. It was Grayson. His life had never been secure. He tilted his chin up and leaned back in the swing, so he looked at Finley upside down. Grayson liked the way it made him lightheaded. "Daddy?"

"Aye, wee one?"

A bright smile snapped to Grayson's lips. Finley knew him too well. He had missed those words. "Can we get married?"

Finley plucked him from the swing, forcing Grayson to meet and hold his stare. "Are you sure you want to be stuck with me forever?"

Grayson held tightly to Finley's neck and toyed with Finley's hair. He nodded. "I've never had a steady home and someone who loves me. Not that I can recall, anyhow. I don't want to be scared anymore."

A slow smile spread across Finley's face. "I love you, but I never thought you'd want to marry me after everything I've done. I worried you'd never trust me that much."

Grayson's eyebrows snapped together. "Of course I trust you. You're my daddy."

Finley's smile somehow grew even bigger. "Let's do it."

A happy squeal burst from Grayson. Their lips met automatically, as if they went for each other at the same time. Pure joy poured through Grayson. He honestly hadn't expected Finley to say yes, much less be enthusiastic about the idea. Grayson thought Finley wouldn't want another husband after Coby. He had been prepared to accept that since he didn't want to replace the man Finley had loved so much. Now he realized Finley loved him equally. It was more humbling than he'd expected. Things turned heated fast. Grayson wondered if he was about to get fucked on a jungle gym.

"I hope you two don't mind the interruption."

Grayson and Finley turned their heads at the sound of Max's voice. Max, Kage, Tommy, Silas, and Benji were waiting for their attention.

Max had a bottle of champagne in each hand and one tucked beneath his arm. "I was in the bushes during your proposal for... reasons and thought this sounded like a good excuse to get fucked up."

"He means celebrate," Benji corrected.

Max nodded. "That too."

Grayson smiled so hard, his cheeks ached as bottles popped and champagne passed from person to person. Before his first invite to one of these events, Grayson had never known acceptance. Never in his wildest dreams could he have foreseen how that would lead to finding so much love. So much fucking love. Grayson's heart overflowed with it. Just like everything in his life, it hadn't come easily. But, for once, it was worth it. His gaze slid toward the love of his life. Finley was worth it. He was imperfect. Just like Grayson. That made them even better together. They would have a great life.

Keep an eye out for the next book in the 'D' series, *Wastrel*.

Please consider leaving a review at the retailer where you purchased this book. Reviews really help with a book's visibility, which allows me to continue writing more stories. Thank you, Charity.

SNUGGLED

About the Author

Charity Parkerson is an award-winning and multi-published author with several companies. Born with no filter from her brain to her mouth, she decided to take this odd quirk and insert it in her characters.

*Eight-time Readers' Favorite Award Winner

*2015 Passionate Plume Award Finalist

*2013 Reviewers' Choice Award Winner

*2012 ARRA Finalist for Favorite Paranormal Romance

*Five-time winner of The Mistress of the Darkpath

Connect with her online:

*Sign up for her newsletter: https://sendfox.com/charityparkerson

*Join her readers' group on Facebook: http://bit.ly/CharitysTribe

*Website: https://www.charityparkerson.com

*A list of her social media accounts and giveaways all in one place: http://hy.page/charityparkerson